I0831519

AWKWARD ABROAD

AN AWKWARD NOVEL

RACHEL RHODES

First published 2019

Cover design by Canva

Edited by The Writer's Block

I wake with a dull pain in my head and the all too familiar dry mouth that follows a night of heavy drinking. I lie as still as possible, knowing that when I move, it's going to bring a world of hurt. Only yesterday I'd sworn off booze. I was going to go dry for a month to give my liver a much-needed break. As it turns out, the road to hell truly is paved with good intentions. I'd lasted all of six hours before Lara suggested a Vodka tonic at *The Appaloosa*.

Tentatively, I turn my head, and a wave of pain cuts through my skull. I can only clutch my forehead until it subsides, cursing my non-existent willpower. In the kingdom of self-destructive assholes, I'm a queen. What I'm not, however, is a masochist. I avoid pain wherever possible, which is why I pull a pillow over my head and go right back to sleep.

The sun is high in the sky when I wake again. The silky softness of satin caresses my skin. I peer below the sheets and utter a low curse. I'm naked. And now that I think about it, I don't have satin sheets. My hand inches across the broad expanse of the bed, terrified I might encounter warm male flesh. I almost weep in relief to discover I'm alone. Through lowered lashes, I examine my surroundings. The hotel suite is impressive, even by my standards. Floor to ceiling windows stretch the length of the wall opposite the bed. Gauzy tulle curtains blow gently in the breeze at the open balcony door. I scan every inch of the room I can see without moving a muscle, and only when I'm almost certain I'm alone, do I lift my head. A discarded champagne flute lies on its side on a marble table. Beyond that rises an enormous white sofa, utterly devoid of any cushions. They're strewn across the pale grey carpet, along with my clothes. The Michael Kors dress I was wearing last night, lies in a crumpled heap next to an empty Moët bottle. The scrap of red lace a few feet away brings a flush to my cheeks.

I flop back onto the satin sheets and drape my arm over my eyes, willing myself to remember what the hell happened last night. I remember doing Tequila shots. I remember holding onto the bar counter when the room started to spin. I'd been with Lara, or at least I had been until that stag party had arrived. After that, everything is a bit of a blur.

"Good morning, Amber." The voice is curt, clipped, and to my horror, utterly familiar. I'd know that voice anywhere. I've heard it almost every day for as long as I can remember. I sit bolt upright and gape at the figure lounging against the balcony door. It feels like I left my brain behind on the pillow, but that's the least of my worries. I'm naked, and this is *his* room. The perfectly logical conclusion is one that I refuse to consider.

"I said good morning, Amber," Kent James repeats dryly, then, after an exaggerated look at his watch, "or perhaps good afternoon would be more appropriate."

Caught quite literally with my pants down, I go immediately on the defensive. "What's so good about it?"

"I guess not much from your position."

"Oh, go and nail your dick to a door."

"Always so eloquent. It's nice to see you putting that private school education to good use."

I'm distracted by the scent of coffee, only to realize he's holding a steaming mug. I glance pointedly at it and arch my brow.

"Oh, sorry," he says, sounding wholly unapologetic as he waves the mug in my direction. "I would have got you one, but I figured from the snoring you'd be asleep a few more hours."

I'm too hungover to think of a suitable response. "What the hell happened last night? Why am I in a hotel room? And why am I naked?" I add, throwing him a filthy look.

He chuckles, low and melodious.

"Firstly, you owe me for the room," he says. "There was no way I'd have made it across town with you in the state you were in when I found you last night." He gives me the stern look which stopped working on me years ago. "And secondly, don't flatter yourself. Every other guy in that club might've wanted a piece of your ass – including the groom to be, by the way, but I prefer my women with a little more self-respect."

It's a low blow, but I let it slide. "So, we didn't actually...?"

"Have sex?"

I grimace. "Ugh. God, Kent, could you be any more gross?"

"Hey, I'm not the one who was tearing my clothes off last night and claiming I'd take you to places you'd only ever dreamed about."

I risk a glance at my crumpled dress. "I didn't."

"Oh, you did. You also drank an entire bottle of Moët, which I'm going to have to pay for."

"You can afford it," I grumble.

"So can you. I'll send you the bill."

"Fine. Now can we just pretend none of this ever happened and go back to annoying each other to death? Throw me my dress so I can get the hell out of here."

An exasperated look crosses his face. It's a nice face, actually. Strong features, but with surprising softness to them when he thinks no one is looking. Those intense green eyes which always make me look away first. No matter how nice the face, though, Kent's been a bit of a dick since college. He's not someone I would associate with by choice, not anymore anyway. The fact that our mothers have been best friends since childhood means that we've known each other, unofficially, since the womb. We were born only two weeks apart and spent most of our childhood giving our mother's grey hairs. Now, Kent works for my father and seems set to become every bit as uptight and intolerant as he is.

My father, Peter Holland, is a property magnate who spends his days terrorizing his massive staff complement and making money. A harsh man who sees everything in black and white, he has never forgiven me for flouting his authority and opting to study language over property law. A strict teetotaller, with an iron will and impeccable self-control, my erratic and irresponsible behavior drives him demented.

In Kent, however, he has found the perfect ally. Not only does he add some much-needed modernism to Saber Development, the company my father started only a few years after I was born, he also dons a twin frown of disapproval every time I so much as set a toe out of line. Which, incidentally, only encourages me further. It wasn't always like this. Growing up, Kent and I were inseparable – the terrible twosome, our mothers had called us. Together, we had wreaked havoc in the lives of the endless slew of nannies charged with trying to keep us under control. In second grade, I'd pummelled the nose of a particularly revolting boy who had made the mistake of trying to bully Kent on the playground. When the teacher on duty had grabbed my hands, I'd landed a well-placed kick to his crotch for good measure. In our sophomore year, a boy that I harbored a thumping crush on had made a lewd comment about my chest in front of the entire cafeteria during recess. By the fifth period, he'd been sporting a spectacular black eye, and Kent was nursing two broken knuckles. I'd told him he forgot to tuck in his thumb, then hugged him until he'd complained he didn't want to add two broken ribs to the list of injuries.

We'd been a team, back then, equally wild and accountable only to each other. We'd set off for college in his trusty Ford, my father having refused to buy me a car after I'd crashed his golf cart into the shed, filled with optimism and excitement. Little did we know that everything was about to change. Within six months, Kent had met a gorgeous blonde undergrad named Erica, who ate tofu and spent her free time hugging trees. I'd laughed at her sanctimonious attitude, but for the first time, Kent hadn't laughed with me. It wasn't long before we began to drift apart. When I joined the most popular drinking club on campus, Kent had joined the student council. Erica didn't last long, but it didn't matter. The seed she had planted continued to bloom, and something between us had been irreparably damaged. By the time we graduated, we were barely on speaking terms.

I left college with a degree, a group of friends who promised to be a lifelong bad influence, and no intention of finding a job anytime soon. Kent, on the other hand, wanted to start working before the ink had dried on his degree. Determined to work his way up the ladder, he'd approached my father for a letter of recommendation, having spent three summers interning at Saber. My father had taken one look at his impressive results, added a healthy dose of nepotism, and offered him a job. He's been wearing tailored suits and oozing disapproval ever since. Daddy's right-hand man, I like to call him these days. Mostly to his face.

"Amber?" It takes me a moment to realize that Kent has been speaking for some time and I haven't heard a word. "Are you even listening to me?"

"I'm trying not to, as far as I can help it."

"You might want to start, this is important."

A sense of unease creeps up my spine. He's wearing the face – the one he only wears when he's about to deliver bad news. The last time I saw it, my dad had insisted I get a job. It only lasted one summer, but I still shudder at the memory.

"Be warned, you're probably going to hate me even more than you do already once you hear this," Kent says.

"Not possible," I grumble, but he's not even listening. He's too caught up in his own rhetoric.

"And just so you know, I didn't want to be the one to tell you this. Not that you don't deserve it, but I'm getting tired of being the mediator between you and your father."

Liar. I bet he enjoys it. "Spit it out, Kent."

He sets down his mug and comes to sit on the edge of the bed. His eyes are hard and determined.

"You've gone too far, Amber," he says simply. "And your father is no fool. You may think you have the wool pulled over his eyes, but he knows exactly what you get up to."

"And what exactly is it that I get up to?" I ask. Kent has never been comfortable discussing my sex-life, and I'll be damned if I make this easy for him. To my astonishment, he doesn't even hesitate.

"You behave like a whore." It's blunt, brutal, and stings more than I care to admit. "Hell," he continues, "if I hadn't hauled your ass up here last night and fended off your not-so-subtle advances, you'd be walking bow-legged this morning."

An ugly heat rises on my cheeks. "You wish. I'd never throw myself at you, and besides, I doubt you'd be able to 'bow' anything."

"Shut up!" he roars. He's off the bed and halfway across the room before I can blink, pacing like a caged tiger. "You give yourself far too much credit. Your father knows exactly what you get up to, your mother too, and you're acting like that's okay? That your parents shouldn't be concerned when you're meeting Lara at least three times a week at *The Appaloosa*. That you get wasted and leave every time with a different man? You're not even remotely selective, so long as they have a hotel room and a platinum card."

When he says it like that, it does sound rather awful, but I refuse to be shamed like some child, especially by him. "You're twisting everything around. I'm just enjoying my youth."

"You're twenty-three! It's time to grow up."

I open my mouth to argue, then remember that my twenty-third birthday was a few weeks ago, and I'd spent most of it in an alcohol-induced haze. "Fine," I snap, "point taken. I'll try to do better."

"It's too late for false promises."

There's that look again. "What exactly are you saying?"

"Your dad has had enough. He gave you a final warning weeks ago, and you haven't paid even the slightest bit of attention."

"I'm not an employee, Kent. A final warning? Please, it's not like he can fire me."

"True. But he can cut you off."

"He would never."

"You crossed the line when you started sleeping with guys from the office. Do you think they keep quiet about that? The biggest feather in their proverbial cap – screwing Peter Holland's daughter."

"That's not fair. I've only slept with a couple of guys from the office, you're making it sound like I screwed the entire IT department!"

"Stuart and Dave *are* the entire IT department."

"Oh."

Kent runs his hands through his all too perfect black hair and lets out an exasperated sigh. When he looks at me again, his face is weary, his eyes softer.

"You're killing him, Amber. The man has a business to run, and you're making him a laughing stock."

My eyes prickle. I pull the sheets higher to hide my bare shoulders. I know I can be reckless. I want to be more than just a party animal, but as soon as I have that first tequila, it's like Amber disappears, and this other person takes control of my body. She's fierce and afraid of nothing. And apparently always horny.

Kent clears his throat. "I'm sorry," he says softly.

Again, that sense of foreboding. Kent never apologizes.

"Sorry for what? What exactly does this mean? Is he sending me to rehab? Is he curbing my allowance?" I pray it's not the last one. I've become accustomed to a certain lifestyle, and I really don't want to have to give it up. Then Kent speaks again, and I wish having my credit card confiscated was the worst of my worries.

"He's sending you to Beijing."

It takes me a full minute to recover. "You can't be serious."

He doesn't falter. "You'll be given enough money for rent and food. The rest you'll have to work for."

"You're not serious," I echo, then, when he doesn't respond, "what the hell am I supposed to do in Beijing?"

"The thing you're qualified to do. I've set up interviews at three different schools. You'll be teaching English, and finally putting that degree to good use."

I want to laugh at the absurdity of what he is saying, but I can't.

"Don't be immature about this," Kent warns, sensing an argument brewing. "Peter has given you plenty of chances to sort yourself out, but you're only getting worse. The last few weeks have been like watching a slow-motion train wreck. Consider this an intervention before you land yourself in serious trouble."

"This is ridiculous. You can't just send me away, I'm not a child."

"Really? You certainly act like one." I don't dignify that with a response, and he relents. "You're a smart girl. You have everything going for you, or at least you did before you became so hell-bent on destroying yourself. Your dad only wants what's best for you. For once in your life, just take his advice and try to be responsible. Who knows, maybe you'll get off early for good behavior."

"I'm not going to Beijing," I insist. "I'm almost certain I have a date tonight, and I plan to keep it."

His face falls. "What happened to you, Amber?" he whispers, so softly I barely catch the words.

I hate it when he does that. Shows a side of him that reminds me of our youth, and acts like he gives a shit. In an attempt to gain some control over the situation, I get out of bed without saying a word, flaunting my naked, sunbed-bronzed body while I leisurely reach for my dress. When I turn to put it on, he's looking the other way. *Bastard.*

With his back still to me, he says, in a voice like flint, "Go take a shower. Make yourself look less like a hooker. There's a boutique downstairs. I'll pick up some clothes for you. Your car leaves for the airport this afternoon."

I throw him a filthy look, grab my purse, and stagger toward the bathroom. Once the door is closed behind me, I rummage for my phone. The battery is almost dead. I sit on the edge of the marble double sink and dial my dad's number. He answers on the first ring.

"Don't even think about trying to change my mind."

"Daddy—"

"Daddy nothing. I am done playing games, Amber. You need to know how seriously I take your future, even if you don't. You can go to Beijing under my terms, or you can give it all up and try to make a life for yourself here with no help from me."

I open my mouth to argue, but he's already cut the call.

When I emerge from the bathroom, feeling marginally more human, Kent is nowhere to be seen, but fresh clothes are draped over the back of the armchair. I pick up each item, marveling at his keen observation. I could've picked this exact outfit from my own closet. Ripped jeans, a grey T-shirt, and an olive-green military style jacket, all a perfect fit. I scowl at the cheap white sneakers I wouldn't be caught dead in. *Asshole.*

Anticipating the glare outside, I don my Tiffany sunglasses before I leave the room. They're also perfect for hiding my bloodshot eyes. I need a plan. There's no way I'm going to China – I can't even hold a chopstick. As soon as I've recovered from my hangover, I'm going to find a way out of this.

I hit the sidewalk and spot a Starbucks on the corner. My pace increases automatically as my caffeine craving re-awakens. Five minutes later, armed with my usual Grande skinny vanilla latte and two bottles of water, my spirits are already lifting. I hand over my card, grateful that the gum-cracking cashier isn't keen on small talk.

She swipes my card and then gives me a look of bored annoyance when it's declined. I've already started on the latte.

"Impossible," I snap. "Try it again."

She does. Declined. Two different cards produce the same result. The cashier grows more tight-lipped by the second as the queue grows behind me. I scrabble in my purse for cash, but I only have five dollars.

"I'll just take the latte," I say, dumping the water on the counter and handing over the crumpled bill.

Humiliated and furious, I'm not even surprised when I walk out of Starbucks to find my father leaning against the black SUV parked across the road. His arms are crossed tightly over his chest. I drag my feet toward him. Not for nothing is my father known as the great white of the development world. Tall and barrel-chested, he oozes natural confidence and charm, but as those who have tried to cross him have learned, his bite is deadly. I fix my eyes on his chest. He's not wearing a tie. A very bad sign. I swallow on the lump which has formed in my throat and rise onto my toes to brush a quick kiss across his jaw.

"Hi, Daddy."

He takes in my wet hair, the dark glasses.

"Take them off," he orders. His voice is strained. I have no choice but to obey, and I wince as the sunlight stabs my eyes.

"Christ."

"Dad—" I prepare to start groveling.

"Get in the car."

"But Daddy—"

"Get in the car!"

I bolt around the SUV and leap into the passenger seat. I haven't felt so terrified since the day he caught me smoking weed behind mom's hydrangea bushes. He folds himself into the driver's seat, and we pull away from the curb.

We drive in silence for about ten minutes. It feels like a lifetime. I try to breathe out of the very corner of my mouth, so he won't be asphyxiated by tequila fumes.

I know the hammer will fall, but I'm not sure when. I sneak a glance across at him, but his face gives nothing away. When he finally speaks, I jump in my seat.

"Did you have fun last night?"

It's not a question which I can answer honestly and live to tell the tale, so I shrug instead.

"You reek of booze."

"I didn't have that much to drink."

"Your credit card bill begs to differ."

"It was Lara's birthday, I was buying rounds."

He spares me a disgusted look and shakes his head. "You're a lousy liar, Amber."

Feeling like I might burst into tears, I mumble, "I'm sorry."

He takes a left turn, his hands perfectly positioned at ten and two.

"Kent explained about Beijing?" he asks once he's straightened out.

"Dad, that's really extreme. I know you're mad at me, but you can't seriously expect me to just up and go to China?"

"I'm surprised you even know where it is."

He's definitely spitting. He's never been so cruel before.

"I'm not an idiot."

"So you only act like one?"

I slump back in my seat. "You're blowing this completely out of proportion. Mom will never agree to this." A few years ago, I might actually have believed it.

"Your mother supports my decision one hundred percent."

What? "Well, I don't! It's my life, and I'm not a child. You can't make me go."

He shoots me a stern look.

"Amber, I have entertained your bad behavior for over two years. At first, I was happy to accept it as a rite of passage after college, but enough is enough. I don't know why you have such a strong desire to sabotage yourself..." I try to interrupt, but he cuts right across me. "I have never discouraged you from experiencing life, and I was happy to foot the bill while you were studying. I even accepted your choice of degree, although you know it wasn't what I wanted. God knows I've given you enough time to grow up and start taking responsibility for your behavior, but you just keep pushing."

We've pulled into my apartment lot, the gorgeous studio apartment that he paid for. He kills the engine and swivels to face me.

"I have put my blood, sweat and tears into building this company so I could give you everything I never had. To offer you a future. And all you've done is take advantage. I wanted to raise an independent, strong-willed woman. Instead, I've raised a spoilt brat."

I flinch away from the hurtful words.

"Please," I whisper, mortification flushing my cheeks. "Please, give me another chance." I rack my brain to think of an alternative that would appease him. "I could come and work for you? I could come and work for Saber, if that's what you want."

He draws in a deep breath. It's what he's always wanted, but I turned my back on that path years ago.

"What I want," he says slowly, "is for you to lead a full and happy life. I want you to become the woman that I know you are, deep down inside. A woman who cares about more than just shoes."

"I do care about things!" I insist, casting a guilty look at the hideous sneakers.

"Like what?" he shakes his head again. "Do you even know what today is?"

"Friday?" I don't mean to say it so flippantly, but the damage is done. His eyes grow dark, and his hands clench into fists on his lap. I sense a storm brewing.

"It's October thirteenth, Amber!"

The significance of that date hits me like a bullet between the eyes. I clap a hand to my mouth. "Oh, God."

His mouth is a grim line and I can't blame him. I'd completely forgotten my mother's birthday.

This time when he speaks, I know there is no hope.

"You will go to Beijing, and you will turn your life around. This is your very last chance. And if I hear you've set one foot out of line, I will withdraw your food and accommodation allowance and let you figure it all out for yourself. I am done enabling you."

It takes me a long time to pack. I'd begged my dad to delay my flight by a day so I could go and see my mom before I left, but he'd refused. "She'll be at the airport to see you off," was all he'd said.

LAX never looked so depressing. I find them waiting for me at departures, my mom trying desperately not to cry. I go straight into her arms, tears of shame pricking at my eyes.

"I'm so sorry, mom," I tell her, and I mean it.

"Let's get you checked in," she replies sadly, "then we'll grab a coffee."

I've always been close with my mom. I certainly get my wilder side from her, although my father keeps hers in better check.

"I need to make a quick call," my dad says once we're seated, and my mother and I share a secret smile. We both know that there's no call – he's just giving us a few minutes alone to say our goodbyes.

"I'm really sorry, mom," I say again, once he's gone.

"You don't have to apologize. These things happen." She says it as if getting drunk and passing out is something that happens *to* one, and not something that one brings upon oneself.

"I don't want to go," I say softly. It's my way of testing the waters, but to my dismay, her lips tighten into a grim line.

"I hate to admit it, sweetheart, but I think your father is right."

"You agree with him?"

"I do." She fixes me with one of her signature glares. "And you *know* how hard that is for me to admit."

I do know. Like I said, my mother can be wild. Kent's mom, Janine, calls her Mustang Sally for good reason. Sometimes I think they allowed Kent and I to get away with murder when we were younger because we reminded them so much of themselves.

"Do you remember that wine tasting we went to at the country club?"

She tries not to smile. "It's hard to forget."

A couple of years ago, I'd joined my mother and Janine on a rare night out. It was for a good cause – all funds raised were donated to charity, although for the life of me I don't remember which one. We'd arrived early, and my mother had managed to charm a complimentary bottle out of the organizers, which we'd polished off in no time. Janine coaxed a second bottle out of them, and then like a lamb, they'd sent me out amidst the wolves to hunt for more. I'd come back with a bottle under each arm and the number of a very cute waiter named Chad. By the time the event was underway, the three of us were smashed. Still, it wasn't my idea to steal that golf cart. Oh no, that blame lay firmly on the shoulders of Mustang Sally and her trusty sidekick.

"It was hilarious, mom. One of the best nights of my life."

My mother's smile fades. "Do you remember how it ended?"

"Of course I do."

My dad and Kent had had to bail us out of the security office at the Country Club, who fortunately didn't press charges due to the fact that Peter Holland is one of their most generous benefactors. I'm still not sure who was more furious – my father, or the security guard who actually caught us removing the 'O' in Country Club from the sign at the main gate.

"Amber, honey, that's exactly what worries me."

"What?"

"That night wasn't something to be proud of. It was fun, sure, but I still cringe whenever I think about it."

"But mom, it was just a little innocent fun!"

"Oh, sweetheart," she sighs, leaning forward to tuck a loose strand of hair behind my ear. "It's all innocent fun. Until it isn't."

AN HOUR LATER, I'm waiting to board. I check my ticket. Economy, go figure. I've never traveled economy in my life. Sandwiched between an elderly man and a sullen teen with a pair of earphones draped around her neck, I resign myself to the fact that there will be no sleeping on this flight.

By the time we land, it feels like someone threw a bucket of gravel into my eyes. I switch on my phone to find a message from Kent: *I've arranged a driver to collect you and take you to your apartment. Safe travels.*

I know that none of this is his fault, but I need someone to blame, and considering this nightmare started in his hotel room, he seems like a worthy recipient.

My reply is a single emoji – the one showing the middle finger. Because I am that mature.

I walk through the arrival terminal to find a sullen Chinese man holding a sign with my name scrawled across it in neon green ink. Or at least I assume, it's my name. It actually reads Am Ba Hole And. *Sweet Jesus.* The man grabs my bag and pumps my hand in a bone-crushing handshake, but he doesn't speak a word to me. I rub at my eyes and follow him out to the waiting car.

The city streaks past in a blur beyond the window. There is beauty here, but it feels cold and unfriendly. When we pull up outside a high-rise apartment block, I gape up at it in alarm. It's hideous. The raw brick has been leached of all color and paint is flaking from the metal window frames. A few rusted satellite dishes hang limply from the wall.

"I think there's been a mistake," I tell the driver, but he only shakes his head and jabs his finger on his GPS device. I peer around, hoping to miraculously find a five-star hotel opposite, but there's only another awful block and a dingy restaurant. This is really happening. I want to turn around and go straight back to the airport. To catch a flight home and throw myself at my father's feet and my mother's mercy.

The driver, who still hasn't spoken a word, dumps my suitcase on the sidewalk and hands me a key. The tag tells me I'm the lucky new tenant of apartment 43.

"Could you...?" I start to ask the driver for assistance with my suitcase, but he's already back in the car. As it pulls away, I fight the urge to run after it. I square my shoulders, realize I can't pull my suitcase in that position, and stoop, admitting defeat. The lobby is empty, and the elevator takes at least four minutes to reach me. It then creaks ominously as it creeps to the fourth floor. I tremble all the way up, praying it doesn't break.

When the doors open, I bolt out of the elevator and onto the most hideous grass-green carpet I've ever seen. It hurts my eyes to look at it.

I see no one. The whole experience is unnerving, as if I've stepped into a cheap Hollywood horror movie. If I get axed to death in this shithole, I'm coming back to haunt Kent. As quickly as I can, I let myself into apartment 43. It's probably identical to every other apartment in the block and could fit into my apartment back home ten times over. I drag my bag into the tiny bedroom and give the miniscule closet a hateful look. I'm too tired to even bother unpacking. Overwhelmed and terrified, I fall onto the scratchy sheets, and try to swallow down the lump in my throat, vowing I won't cry. The past twenty-four hours barely seems real. I am all alone, over 6,000 miles from home. And I have no idea how I am going to survive the next few minutes, let alone a whole year. I close my eyes and try to imagine that I'm back home, curled up in my own bed. I dream of satin sheets.

I wake to a thunderous banging. It takes a few seconds to register where I am, another couple to force down the depression that follows. Stumbling to the door, I open it to find a short Chinese man grinning broadly up at me.

"Hurro, Miss Amber! I here to take you to Engrish."

My first impulse is to tell him to piss off, but if there is any hope of me getting my life back, I need to at least prove to my Dad that I tried. I step aside and wave him in.

"Mister Kent text you, yes?"

I check, to find that yes, Mr. Kent had indeed texted me. *I've arranged for transport to your interviews, he'll be there at 7.*

"I'm going to change," I say, gesturing at my rumpled clothes. He bobs his head twice, grin still firmly in place.

I'm showered and dressed in under twenty minutes, quite possibly a record. I've scraped my hair back into a ponytail and slapped some tinted moisturizer on my face, but I don't bother with any more make-up than a coat of mascara and smear of lip gloss.

My driver is waiting exactly where I left him, teeth in full view. How anyone can smile that wide for that long, is beyond me. I can barely see his eyes, they're so scrunched up in his face.

"I take you to interviews now, Miss Amber. I hope your Engrish better than mine, or you fucked."

Whoever taught him to speak English obviously missed a few very important rules. I burst out laughing but halfway through it turns into a sob. His smile vanishes, replaced by a look of alarm.

"Miss Amber, you okay?"

I give a groan of despair and press my fingers into my temples to ward off the headache I can feel coming on. "I'm fine," I mumble. "What should I call you?" He falters. "Your name," I say slowly, pointing at his chest.

He beams, understanding dawning. "Denri," he says, mimicking the gesture and jabbing at his own chest. "Denri Wu." Then, without missing a beat, "we go now, traffic bad."

Denri drives a compact Volkswagen. I find myself clutching the sides of my seat as he zips through downtown traffic. He wasn't lying about it being bad. Over the honk of horns, I try to catch a glimpse of my new home. It still doesn't look very welcoming. Every now and again, Denri mutters under his breath in Mandarin. For all his clumsy charm, he shifts the little car like a pro.

"How long have you been a driver?" I ask.

He flashes his teeth. "No driver. Favor for Mister Kent."

"How exactly do you know Kent?"

"Mister Kent do work."

Well, that sums it up. "He works with you?"

He shakes his head. Scrunches up his eyes in concentration. "You father?"

"My father?" Furious head bobbing. I try to recall a single time I've heard of Saber doing business in China but draw a complete blank. I'm embarrassed to admit how little I know about my father's company, especially considering that up until now it has funded my lavish lifestyle.

Denri pulls up beside a school playground and kills the engine. "You go. I wait."

A few kids wave as I walk past on my way toward what I hope is the administration block. I wave back, fighting down a growing dread. I can barely communicate with Denri, what if it's the same here? Plus, I'm still jetlagged. The whole experience feels surreal.

Fortunately, the principal speaks remarkably good English. I answer his questions as well as I can, and the interview goes by without a hitch. My lack of teaching experience is a concern, he tells me, but my credentials are perfectly acceptable. He promises he'll be in touch.

The second interview is a disaster. The Dean has been called away on an unexpected emergency, so I'm interviewed by a whippet-slim British girl who has been teaching at this school for over a year.

One look at her, and I know the instant dislike is mutual. She proceeds to fire a volley of questions at me, all of which feel more like an English exam than a job interview. Halfway through, I stifle a yawn and get to my feet.

"Thank you for your time," I say.

"We're not done," she sputters.

"Yeah, we are."

"It go good?" Denri asks as I slump into the passenger seat.

"It go great!" I lie.

The third interview is the most promising. It's an International English school, and the Dean is a petite Chinese woman in her mid-thirties who introduces herself as Bianca and speaks with an American accent.

"You're American!" I gasp before I can help myself.

"Born and raised in Chicago," she confirms with an easy laugh. "My parents moved there before I was born. They named me Bianca and figured I'd fit right in – as if it would be that easy. As if no one would notice my last name was Chen."

"How did you end up back here?" I ask, genuinely curious.

"I've been back and forth a few times, but China has always felt more like home. My grandmother lives just down the street, and my cousin's children come to this school."

"And your parents?"

"Still in the US," she shrugs. "They're divorced now."

"So much for the American dream."

"Tell me about it."

The rest of the interview is easy and natural. Bianca is more interested in my skill-set than any teaching experience I may or may not have had, and I can tell that she likes me. She promises to let me know the outcome within a week. I leave with a sense of pride that I haven't felt in years, and wave far more enthusiastically at the children as I pass the playground on the way to the car.

Denri drives me back to my apartment. Picking up on my positive attitude, he praises me for a job well done, and I don't have the heart to point out that he would hardly know given that he spent the entire time in the car. He walks me right to the elevator before he hands me his business card, with strict instructions to call him if I need anything, no matter the time, day or night. At least, that's what I think he said. He could well have been giving me a recipe for Dim Sum.

Upstairs, I decide not to tempt fate by texting my dad that I may have found a job. Instead, I Google the nearest takeaway restaurants and order in. My credit card payment goes through.

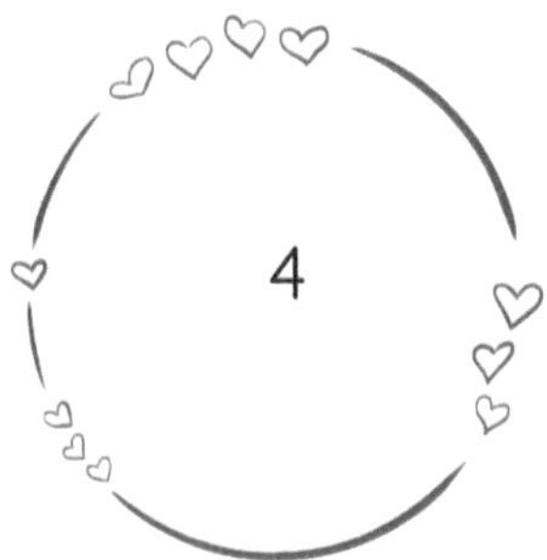

I sleep for fourteen hours straight and wake feeling better able to cope, but with a crick in my neck –a combination of cattle-class travel, and the rock-hard mattress adorning my new bed. Not just a new bed, but a new life. I still can't quite process everything that's happened in the past few days, but after a solid night's sleep, I feel a sudden need to prove myself, or at least, to prove everyone else wrong. I know I haven't got a job offer yet, but this might actually work out. Who knows, maybe I'll be home sooner than I think. I'm sure my father will see sense once he's over his latest tantrum.

I almost don't recognize the tone when my phone rings. Vaulting out of bed, I scrabble in my purse until I find it. Lara's name flashes on the screen. All thoughts of making it on my own vanish.

"Hey!" I answer, so excited to hear a familiar voice I could cry.

"Get your dancing shoes on, you sexy bitch," Lara commands. "We're going out."

I've never been great at math, but I'm pretty sure it's early evening back home. I frown at the morning sunlight streaming through the cheap curtains of my apartment and then slump back on the bed. "I can't. You're not going to believe me when I tell you this, but I'm in China."

"China?" she squawks. "What the hell are you doing in China?"

"It's a long story. Believe me, I'd rather be there."

"Well get your sweet arse on a plane and get back here, then!"

"I can't. My dad's put his foot down. I have to stick it out."

Lara wails. "How am I supposed to have any fun without you?"

"I'm sure you'll do just fine," I tease, thinking that we may start our evenings together, but we seldom end them that way.

"I'm serious, Ambs. I *need* you."

"Why?" I laugh. "You're perfectly capable of causing trouble all on your own."

"Yeah, but..." she trails off and it occurs to me that she might need me for a reason I haven't considered. In all the times Lara and I have partied together, she's never once picked up a tab. It never bothered me because I'd been spending my father's money, and people in glass houses shouldn't throw stones. But suddenly, it does bothers me. A lot. I choose my next words carefully, praying I'm wrong.

"Lara, I hate to ask but all my accounts have been frozen and–" I begin, but Lara is already backpedaling.

"Sweetie, I'm so sorry, but I have to go. I didn't realize you were abroad, this call must be costing me a fortune."

"Actually, I think I"

"Call me the second you get back! Love you madly, sassy pants!"

I blink at my phone, watching as the screen fades to black. She hung up. That lying, using bitch hung up on me. Deep down, I think I always knew that Lara wasn't a true friend, but it still stings to be proven right.

WITH NOTHING else to do and only my foul mood for company, I set out on my own to explore and familiarise myself with my new neighborhood. I discover a bunch of takeaway restaurants just a few streets down from mine, and a 24-hour liquor store, which I scurry past as fast as I can. I can't afford to make that kind of mistake, literally can't afford it, now that my father has set a strict limit on my credit card. It occurs to me that I didn't actually think to check what that limit is.

I walk until my feet hurt, determined to embrace the culture of a new and interesting city. The streets are buzzing with people, and the air is not as clean as I'm used to. When I stumble into an informal market, I'm assailed by the smell of fish and spices, cheap plastic, and cat piss. A grizzled woman with a leathery face offers me a plate piled high with chicken feet, and I bolt, weaving through stalls as though the hounds of hell are after me. I emerge on the other side of the market and take a few deep, steadying breaths. So much for immersing myself in the culture. Across the street, I spot a bicycle hiring stand. Perfect! My feet are killing me, and I'll cover far more ground on a bike. I navigate the docking station quickly, sparing only a fleeting concern for the sixty-dollar charge to my credit card. It's refundable, and besides, there's no way my father can find fault with me hiring a bicycle to get around, it's healthy cardio.

It takes me about half a mile and several near misses with startled pedestrians before I find my balance. I can't remember when last I rode a bike, but I guess it's true what they say about never forgetting. I coast down street after street, finding my rhythm and getting hopelessly lost, when suddenly the city begins to fall away. Gone are the high-rise buildings and, in their place, stand temple-like structures, with intricate artwork carved into their walls. It's greener here, the air thinner, easier to breathe. I pedal slowly, taking it all in, and then I follow a crowd of people who all seem to be walking in the same direction until I find myself at the southern gate of the Forbidden City, which I recognise from the tourist signboard I saw on the way from the airport. I stare in wonder at the stone expanse, the five arches, and the sight takes my breath away. Wordlessly, I park the bicycle in a designated area and join the queue. I hand over my credit card to pay the entrance fee, not caring if I don't eat for a week.

The massive entrance leads into a large area surrounded by the same beautiful buildings. There is an awed hush, a respectful silence as visitors simply stand and stare at the palatial architecture. And then, a loud, nasal voice shatters the quiet. I whirl around in a fury to find a portly tour guide wearing Ray-Bans and leather sandals, surrounded by a crowd of tourists kitted out with selfie-sticks and fanny packs.

"... used to be the imperial palace in the Ming and Qing Dynasties, and ordinary people were not allowed in without permission," the guide is saying now. He pauses, and I sense a punchline in the making. I cringe as he opens his mouth. "But don't worry, we won't kick you out. You all paid the entrance fee!" *What an asshole.* The polite half of the crowd forces fake laughter, while the rest pretend not to have heard. I meet the eyes of a blond girl about my age, and she rolls hers, displaying an alarming amount of white. I give her a sympathetic look and then can't help but grin. As the guide waxes lyrical about the history of the Meridian Gate, through which they've just come, I wander off in the opposite direction. It feels ironic, standing here in this hallowed place – the banished daughter sent to the Forbidden City for her sins – and yet, as far as punishment goes, this isn't the worst thing that could have happened. I'd never have made it here myself, never have experienced the beauty and wonder of this glorious place. I might even have to stop hating Kent.

"You seem quite in awe of the Forbidden City." A deep voice interrupts my thoughts. A cute, twenty-something, with a deep tan and a mop of curly brown hair, is standing beside me. My eyes come to settle on the loudest floral shirt I've seen since a trip to Hawaii a few years back.

I shrug. "I was just wondering why I bothered to climb the wall to get in when the gate is wide open." It's a joke worthy of the loud-mouthed tour guide, but to my astonishment, he throws back his head and laughs, as if he finds my response genuinely funny.

"Nice shirt," I tease, warming to him instantly.

He looks down at it. "It's amazing, right? I won it in a dare."

"Was the dare to wear it in public?"

He flashes me a grin and gazes up at the palace looming above us. "This place is amazing though, right?"

"It is pretty incredible," I admit. "I haven't been this still in a long time."

He turns to face me and thrusts out his hand. "I'm Ben."

I shake his hand. "Amber."

"That's pretty. Like the color."

I shrug. "If you like brown, I guess."

We fall into another pensive silence, only this time, my sense of calm isn't quite as zen as it was a few minutes ago. I'm acutely aware that there is a very handsome boy at my side who laughs at my jokes and is a serious threat to all my good intentions.

"So," Ben says, breaking the silence. "Are you here on a spiritual journey?"

"Something like that."

"Does this spiritual journey allow you any sabbaticals. A drink with me, for instance?"

He really is ridiculously cute.

"That depends."

"On what?"

I think of the splendor which awaits me if I continue to explore the Forbidden City. I think of my father's ultimatum, of Kent's haughty disapproval. I remember the ridiculous limit on my platinum card.

"On who's buying."

THE *JUICY BAR* is only a ten-minute drive from the Forbidden City and is already filled with people and buzzing with conversation and laughter. It seems to be a popular place for tourists because I see hardly any locals in the confined space.

I learn that Ben is originally from San Diego but is currently working his way across the globe with two of his friends, in search of the perfect wave. Josh and Garrett arrive a few minutes after we've settled into a booth and proceed to tear Ben apart for visiting the Forbidden City instead of joining them at the beach. They speak almost exclusively about surfing, which at least accounts for the ridiculously dark tans, but after an hour of *gnarly*, *dude*, and *right on*, I'm ready for something stronger than the beer I've been nursing.

Fortunately, Ben senses my discomfort and gently guides the conversation in other directions. The beer flows fast and furious, and after what must be my fourth draught, I excuse myself to go to the bathroom. I squint at the red tiles which stretch from floor to ceiling, broken only by a garish gold in the form of two enormous mirrors over the sink. The entire effect is revoltingly vulgar. As is my face, I realize in horror, when I catch sight of my reflection. My mascara is smudged beneath my eyes, and my hair is escaping its ponytail. I remove the hair tie and run my fingers through it, then smear a layer of concealer beneath my eyes. It's hot as hell in here. I use the paper towels to wipe my sweaty armpits, then weave my way back to the booth where another full draught awaits.

Ben is eager to know more about me, but I'm not willing to spill the daddy-cut-off-my-credit-card beans, so instead, I fabricate an elaborate story of how hard I've been working, building up my property development company, and how I just needed to get away from it all to center myself.

"You know what you need?" Josh asks, and I squint at his blond dreadlocks.

"What?"

"A tequila!"

Before I know it, the waitress arrives with four tequilas and places them in the middle of the table. I eye the lemon and tug my lower lip between my teeth. I know the right thing to do. I know I have to say no.

"Amber? You okay?" Ben's eyes are crossing, his tousled hair standing on all ends, but when he smiles, my heart flip flops in my chest.

"I'm fine." I snatch up a glass and hold it aloft. "Cheers!"

My mouth is dry, my head throbbing. A hangover. I have a hangover, but somehow it feels worse in China. Maybe it's the altitude. Or maybe I'm just out of practice. The sounds of the street below seem amplified, too, as if every resident of Beijing decided to use the street outside my apartment block as a thoroughfare today. Honking horns, people shouting, doors banging. It's a cacophony of pain, and I pull my pillow over my head with a whimper of frustration.

"Oh good, you're up."

I freeze at the sound of that low, melodious voice. I keep deadly still, praying I imagined it.

"Good morning, Amber."

Son of a bitch! I twist my neck and peer around the pillow. Kent's wicked green eyes gaze back at me. He's standing beside the bed, an open Manila folder in his hands.

"Please tell me I'm just having a really bad case of déjà vu," I groan.

He closes the folder with a snap and shoves it into the laptop bag beside my bed. "No such luck, unfortunately," he says. He looks tired, his suit rumpled as if he slept in it. A five o'clock shadow darkens his jaw, and his face is creased.

"Amber," he begins wearily. "Do you remember anything that happened last night?"

I close one eye, racking my brain, but there are holes in my memory. I remember the Forbidden City, and Ben of the revoltingly loud shirt.

"The Juicy Bar!" I announce in triumph as the name comes back to me. "That's where I went last night."

"Uh-hmm," Kent drawls, sounding far from impressed. "And what time was that?"

"I don't know, around six?"

"I found you wandering around down the street at 4 am," Kent says.

"That can't be right." I do the mental calculation. What in God's name could I have been doing for over eight hours?

"What are you doing here, anyway?" I snap, going on the defensive. "Spying on me?"

"Actually, I had absolutely no intention of even letting you know I was here. I flew in yesterday morning and had back-to-back meetings. You weren't on my list of priorities."

"And yet here you are," I reply smugly.

"I'm here," he thunders, "because the accounts department called me about irregular activity on your credit card. I told them not to tell your dad," he adds menacingly, "until I could get to the bottom of it."

I sit bolt upright in bed, clutching the sheet to my chest.

"What? That's bullshit. I've hardly spent a cent since...." I trail off, the details of yesterday coming back to me.

Kent's nostrils flare, inhaling the scent of victory. "You want to tell me where I can find the bicycle that Shu Cycles claim you stole?"

A COUPLE of Tylenol and a cold shower later, I emerge from the bathroom to find Kent flipping through the Manila folder, his foot tapping in irritation. He's made the bed, which he's sitting on. I don't think I'd ever be able to get it that straight.

"Feel better?" he asks, taking pity on my pale-faced shakiness.

"A little."

He gets to his feet and puts the folder back before shouldering his laptop bag.

"Let's go."

The plush interior of his hired car is heaven, and I melt into the dove-grey leather.

"How come you get a car, and I have to taxi everywhere?"

"Because I'm here on business," he snaps. "It's called a perk, and it generally comes with earning your keep. You should try it sometime."

"God, can you just not," I grumble. "Why do you always have to turn everything into a life lesson? You used to be fun, you know. About a hundred years ago."

He shoots me a warning look. "Fun? Is that what you call what you were up to last night?"

Given that I can't actually remember what I was up to last night, I wisely stay silent.

"That's what I thought," Kent says. He indicates left, makes a perfect turn, and then glances across at me. When he speaks again, there's something different in his voice, a cold fury that I shrink away from.

"I found you wandering the streets, out of your mind, Amber. With three men who seemed thrilled at the prospect of spending the night at your place."

"They were just friends. It wasn't like that."

"You were hardly in any state to be sure of that."

"How did you find me, anyway?"

"I tracked your phone. When I couldn't find you at the apartment, I got worried. Especially knowing you'd hired a bike and hadn't returned it."

"You tracked my phone?" I'm outraged.

"Saber pays your bill," he reminds me darkly. "And before you get on your high horse, I was worried. For all I knew you'd been hit by a car."

"Well, I wasn't. You must be so disappointed."

"God, you're impossible."

"And you're an asshole."

His jaw tightens. "Maybe, but at least I give a shit about you, which is more than I can say for the company you keep. I don't even know why I bother. I should just call your father and tell him you're a lost cause so he can stop wasting his time and money."

"Go ahead. At least I'd get out of this crappy country. It's awful here."

"Bullshit! You're in one of the most beautiful cities in the world, if you'd only take the time to appreciate it."

"I tried," I retort, as we round another corner and the Forbidden City looms into view. "I came here yesterday, in case you've forgotten."

I'm out of the car the second Kent parks, and I scan the area for the bicycle.

"There it is," I say, spotting it amongst a group of bicycles in a nearby stand. "Exactly where I left it."

Kent loads the bike with difficulty into the backseat of the car and we drop it back at the vendor. He pays the fine with his platinum credit card.

"You're paying me back," he says. "The second you get your first paycheck. Now come on, I'll take you to breakfast. We're going to do some straight talking."

"Do we ever do any other kind?"

"Only when you're dead drunk and making inappropriate advances."

He half-smiles, and I can't help but marvel at how it completely transforms his face, so different from the permanent scowl he usually wears in my presence.

"You should smile more," I tell him. "It makes you seem almost human. You might even find yourself a girlfriend."

THE RESTAURANT IS SMALL, a quiet place with rickety wooden tables and chairs upholstered in a cat-sick yellow velvet, and to my delight, the menu is in English. Dark blue paneling lines the walls, and the ancient candelabras cast a soft, warm light over us. Kent clears his throat, and I look away from the ceiling to meet his green eyes.

"They serve vanilla lattes," he tells me wryly. "You want one?"

"I want four."

Kent orders eggs – poached – on rye, but I need grease. He raises a brow when I order a double cheeseburger with fries, but I ignore him, giving a soft sigh of satisfaction as I take a sip of my latte.

He watches me intently, waiting, and eventually, I cave. "I'm sorry," I mumble, setting my mug on the table.

"For what, exactly?"

"You're really not going to make this easy on me, are you?"

He shrugs and crosses his arms over his chest.

"For finding me last night," I admit. "I guess I got in a little over my head. But," I add, throwing him an indignant look, "I wasn't planning on taking anyone to bed. I just... well, it was nice to have company."

"You're lonely?" he asks. "Amber, you've barely been here two days."

"You know me. I don't like being on my own."

"I won't deny that you're a social creature." He's teasing me now, and I roll my eyes.

"You used to be social too, remember?"

"Can I ask you something?"

"You just did." It's my standard reply.

"You're always reminding me of what I used to be. Why does it matter so much?"

"I don't know." I chew on a fry while I think. "I guess because we used to be friends."

"You don't think we're friends anymore?"

I laugh at that. "We haven't been friends since you started dating Erica Gilmore in freshman year and turned into a pretentious prick."

His mouth twitches, but he doesn't comment.

"What did you see in her, anyway?" I ask, through a mouthful of bun. "She was awful."

"She was interested," he replies enigmatically. "And I like how you've turned it all around in your head. Typical Amber, always the victim."

"I *was* the victim. You're the one who changed."

"I'm surprised you even noticed."

"What's that supposed to mean?"

He shakes his head. "It doesn't matter. It's in the past. What I'm concerned about right now is how you plan to get yourself out of this mess."

"Would it help if I said that I genuinely want to prove that I can do it?"

"It might. Depends if you're serious. Last night wasn't exactly reassuring."

"Last night was a mistake. A lapse in judgment. And I can't even promise it won't happen again."

"Well, at least you're being honest," he concedes. "How did the interviews go? Denri said you seemed positive."

"I won't know until I hear."

"Well, keep me posted. If none of those work out, I have a few other contacts I can call in favors from."

It grates me that he'd need to. In that moment, I decide that I'm going to find myself a job if it kills me, with no help from Kent.

"That won't be necessary. I'll do this myself."

"You're so stubborn," he says, but there's a hint of something almost like pride in his voice.

He drops me back at my apartment, and I savor every mile of luxury transport.

"Do you want to come up?" I ask. The words are a surprise, even to me. I guess I just can't face the prospect of spending the rest of the day alone. With myself. "We can watch a movie. They have subtitles, although, I guess you wouldn't need them," I add, recalling that Kent speaks fluent Mandarin.

"I can't. I have a plane to catch."

"You're going back so soon?" I feel a flare of panic at losing my only contact with home.

"Yes. Your father needs my report, and I actually do have a job to do. One that doesn't entail fireman's lifting your drunken ass up four flights of stairs." He winks at me to soften the blow, and I shake my head in mild amusement.

"There's an elevator," I point out.

"Yes, I'm aware." He doesn't offer any further explanation and leaves me standing on the pavement, perplexed, as he drives away.

6

I hate subtitles, I discover, as I lounge on the ancient brown sofa, which is as uncomfortable as it looks. I'm just dozing off when my phone rings with an incoming Facetime call. My mother's face takes up the entire screen on my iPhone. I smile at the sight of her sharp platinum bob and cornflower blue eyes, narrowed in concentration.

"Hi, Mom," I say. As always, she looks astonished to see my face, as though she can't believe the call actually worked. Video calling is definitely a millennial thing.

"Hello, darling!" There's a slight delay and then, "You look exhausted, are you sick?"

There's no way I'm admitting to a hangover. "No, just tired. I think I'm still jetlagged."

"How are you enjoying your trip?" she asks, as if I'm off on some exotic vacation, and haven't been banished to the ass end of the world.

"It's been great so far," I say, knowing better than to correct her. "I've done some sight-seeing, and I've been to three job interviews."

"How did they go?"

"Good, I think. It's hard to tell."

"I'm sure they loved you."

I force a smile. "I hope so."

"Did Kent come and see you? Janine mentioned he was over there on business."

"He did!" I say brightly, knowing it's what she wants to hear. "We had lunch today, it was great."

Her smile is dazzling. "Oh, good! I'm so glad he could find time to fit you in. Your father said he probably wouldn't be able to, with the amount of work he had to get done in such a short space of time."

I ignore the twinge of guilt I feel that Kent had to come to my rescue when he obviously had so much on his plate.

My mother's face disappears as an incoming call shows on my screen.

"Mom, I have to go, I've got another call. It might be from one of the schools."

"Okay," she sounds disappointed. "Let me know if you hear anything positive! I'll be holding thumbs!"

"I will, I promise. Love you, bye!" I switch calls. "Hello?"

"Hello, is this Amber Holland?"

"Yes, speaking."

"Hi Amber, it's Bianca, from the International English school. We met the other day," she adds, unnecessarily. "I was just phoning to let you know that your application was successful."

"What?"

She gives a low laugh at my stunned tone. "We'd like to offer you the teaching position," she says, "that is, if you're still interested?"

"I am most definitely still interested," I say, barely taking in her explanation that I will be starting on Monday morning, and will undergo a brief induction before diving right in. Lesson plans will be provided, thank God.

"The kids are so excited to meet you," Bianca finishes.

"Not as excited as I am," I lie. The prospect of managing a bunch of six-turning-seven-year-olds leaves an oily slick in my gut.

"Thank you," I say before she ends the call. "I really appreciate you giving me the opportunity."

"You're most welcome," she says. "I won't see much of you, except at faculty meetings, but we have some wonderful teachers, and I'm sure you'll fit in well."

The second she's off the line, I text my mom to let her know the good news. I pull up Kent's number, remember that he's on a plane, and set my phone aside.

DENRI ARRIVES twenty minutes early on Monday morning, bursting with excitement as if my landing this job is a personal triumph.

"You knock them down dead, Miss Amber," he grins when he drops me at the school.

"Thanks, Denri." I grin right back, then smooth down my black pencil skirt and square my shoulders.

The school is made up of simple rows of classrooms, situated behind the administration building, and a few playing fields. Bianca meets me in the reception area with a polite but brief apology that she has meetings to attend, and then hands me over to an Australian woman named Mandy, who has been teaching at the school for six months. Her sandy-blonde hair has a gorgeous natural wave and her eyes are a light hazel, warm and welcoming. She's almost my height and has the toned, compact figure of a woman who's been blessed with good genes.

She speaks so quickly that I can barely understand her accent, but I learn that the teaching staff is a mish-mash of foreigners from all over the world, some who joined only a few weeks ago and others who have been here for over five years. I can also tell, within five minutes of being in her company, that Mandy and I are going to get along. She's easy-going, with a wicked sense of humor, and she doesn't take herself too seriously. While we talk, she strides around the admin building, giving me a whirlwind tour.

"God, I hate orientation," she announces, opening a door halfway down the hall. She waves me in first. "Let's get this over with, shall we? I'm sure we don't need to cover *everything*. If you come unstuck, you can just ask."

We spend only about half an hour going through the educator's handbook, which covers teaching methods, the code of conduct, and disciplinary procedures, and then Mandy breathes a sigh of relief. "Time to dive in." She deposits a heavy file intro my arms. "Syllabus." And then, at my look of alarm, "you'll figure it out."

I almost make a run for it when we reach my classroom. Children are tearing around inside, all talking at once. As I watch through the window, a cherubic-looking girl with curly blonde hair and enormous baby blues gives her classmate – a slight, dark-haired boy, a savage pinch. The boy rounds on her, wide-eyed and furious, and then promptly tackles her to the floor. A frazzled looking woman, who must be a temp, hauls him off and sends them both to opposite corners of the room for time out.

"Oh, God," I breathe, watching the chaos unfold from behind the relative safety of the louvered window.

"They're a treat, right?" Mandy laughs, rolling her eyes. "Whoever said teaching is a gift was on meth."

I try to look amused and fail dismally.

"You'll be fine," Mandy says. "Just don't let them know you're terrified. They can smell fear."

"Good to know." I straighten my shoulders and put on my strictest face. Mandy cocks her head to one side.

"Nailed it. I'll see you at lunch!"

"If I survive that long."

"You'll be *fine*," she repeats, and then she's sashaying down the hall, her long skirt flapping behind her.

THE TEMP'S CRY OF, 'Oh, thank God you're here!' the second I step into the classroom, does little to boost my confidence.

How is it possible that there are only twelve children, I think hysterically, trying to do a head count.

An hour later, I'm already frazzled. Being an international school, most of the students are European – children of ex-pats currently living in China. But I do have two native Chinese students – a shy, serious little girl called Li Na, who seems most comfortable in the storybook corner of the room, as far from the other kids as she can get, and Wei Li – the dark-haired, beautiful and unruly boy who tackled the blond girl this morning. Wei is wild, with a capital W. He also spends the entire morning conversing with me exclusively in Mandarin, much to my shock and horror. It's almost lunchtime when I overhear him carrying on an entire conversation with another student in perfect English and realize I've been had.

Fortunately, lunch is provided by the school. It's the same food the children are served in the cafeteria, but I at least get to eat in the staff room, which is mercifully child-free.

"Amber!" Mandy flags me down, and I weave through the tables to sink gratefully onto a chair beside her.

"Hungry?" she asks, eyeing my plate, which is piled high with chicken and noodles.

"One less meal to budget for," I tell her gleefully.

"Clever." She offers me a wicked grin and then turns to a tiny, delicate woman with pale skin and a Halle Berry haircut, who is sitting opposite me.

"Kate, Amber," Mandy says, bits of spinach flying from her crammed mouth. "Amber, Kate."

"Hi!" I extend my hand, and Kate takes it shyly. If first impressions are anything to go by, this girl is as mild as milk. "Have you been working here long?" I ask.

"Just over a month," she replies, her accent instantly recognizable.

"You're British?"

She nods. "I'm from Windsor."

"I adore the U.K," I say, "but only in summer. I can't bear the cold."

"We get that a lot. And you're American?" she asks politely.

"Yeah. California. I love it, it's warm," I tease, and I'm rewarded with a small smile.

"How's your first day going?" Mandy interrupts.

"So far, so good. A few of the kids are..." I try to find a suitable word and fail. "Energetic," I finish, lamely.

Mandy laughs out loud and gives Kate a pointed look. "She's got Wei."

Kate's look of sympathy is utterly genuine.

"Did he pretend he couldn't speak English?" Mandy asks.

"Yes!"

"It's his favorite trick. He's an absolute shit."

"I feel sorry for him," Kate interjects softly, and Mandy rolls her eyes.

"You're such a drip." She's teasing, though, and Kate doesn't look offended. Their dynamic is relaxed, with the easy banter of two people who clicked instantly. Mandy is extroverted and easily bored, whereas Kate seems more shy but self-assured in her own quiet way.

"Wei's parents are super successful," Mandy explains. "You know the type – investment banking and international travel, corporate dining, Louis Vuitton, and rubbing shoulders with the who's who of high society, but taking absolutely zero interest in their own kid."

I feel slightly less hostile toward the little boy who, an hour ago, I was ready to throttle.

"He plays up to get attention," Kate adds, "but admittedly, it's exhausting. I think he just needs someone to pay an interest in him."

"He needs someone to pour some Ritalin in him," Mandy corrects, before turning back to me. "How are you enjoying Beijing so far?"

"I haven't really done much, I've only been here a couple of days. I did go through to the Forbidden City, though," I add, purely to impress.

"Godawful shite," Mandy says, at the same time that Kate lets out an appreciative "Ah, isn't it beautiful?"

"A bit of a culture-vulture is our Kate," Mandy explains. "I, on the other hand, prefer to spend my free time doing *fun* things."

"Sight-seeing *is* fun!" Kate insists, but she's laughing.

I sit back and feel the thrill of possibility wash over me. I like these girls. I *really* like them – they're hilarious and just straight up *nice*. Is it possible I might actually make some friends here? Friends who don't need a platinum card to buy their loyalty?

"We should go out after work," Mandy is saying now. "To celebrate surviving your first day. I know an amazing little pub just down the road."

My first instinct is to balk, but I don't. I might be wanting to turn my life around, but that doesn't mean I have to stop having fun. If anything, this is a chance to prove to myself that I can control myself. An exercise in moderation.

"Sounds good," I say. Mandy grins, and we both turn to face Kate just as the bell rings, signaling time to head back to class.

"Well, obviously I'm in," Kate says, giving Mandy a sidelong glance. "I mean it's not like you're going to give me any choice."

"I'm not," Mandy says, giving a whoop. "I'll meet you both at the main gate after school. Good luck, Amber!" she adds, giving me a wink.

7

Back in the classroom, I find myself watching Wei far more closely than before. He truly is a beautiful child, with thick, sooty lashes and a cupid bow mouth, but his eyes are hooded, solemn, and his destructive behavior is even more obvious now that I'm paying attention. Twice, I catch him striking out at other children with sharp fingers when he thinks no one is looking. More specifically, when he thinks *I'm* not looking.

"Wei," I call, once I've settled the class with their sentence blocks, and his angry eyes cut to me. "Could you come up here, please."

His small body is stiff as a board as he approaches, but I keep a calm smile plastered on my face until he comes to a halt before my desk.

"Wei," I say, speaking softly so the others won't hear. "We don't use our hands to resolve conflict, we use our words." I catch myself, wondering if he even understands the big words I'm using, given his age and the fact that English is his second language. "If I catch you hurting the other children again, I'm going to have to report you to

Principal Chen," I finish. I'm sure the word Principal is easy enough to grasp.

He shrugs as if he couldn't care less. Almost as if he's daring me to do it. I don't rise, and I wave him back to his seat. Not a minute later, Joshua, a sweet little boy sitting on Wei's left, gives a howl of anguish. Wei keeps his eyes fixed on his work as I rush across, only to find a red mark blossoming on Joshua's ribs.

"He did it!" Gabby, the curly-haired blonde points an accusatory finger in Wei's face. Wei slaps it away, then kicks out at Gabby's chair legs, sending her crashing to the floor. Gabby bursts into tears.

"Wei!" I scold, lifting Gabby and her chair and setting them upright. "Outside, right now!"

I settle Joshua and Gabby as quickly as I can and then stalk outside. I walk right past Wei, who is perched on top of a low wall, swinging his legs so hard that his sneakers ram the wall with every kick.

"I'll deal with you in a minute," I tell him over my shoulder as I pass. He doesn't even acknowledge that I've spoken, and I hurry down the hall, peering into every classroom along the way. I heave a sigh of relief as Kate's familiar face comes into view.

"Amber?" she asks when I open her classroom door. "Is everything okay?"

I wait until I'm right beside her before I speak, so her students won't overhear our conversation. "Could you keep an eye on my class for a few minutes? I need to take Wei to Bianca's office."

"That didn't take long." She winces. "What did he do?"

"He physically attacked two kids, after I'd warned him not to."

"Sounds like Wei. Sorry," she adds, catching sight of my stricken expression, "it's just that he generally does the opposite of what he's told. Telling him *not* to do something is basically a guarantee that he will."

"Should he even be in this school? Why hasn't he been expelled, if his behavior is so deviant?"

"It's a long story, but let's just say his parents aren't the kind of people you want on your bad side. Bianca tried to address Wei's issues when he first started here, and they threatened to report her to the education board."

"For what?"

"Racism, would you ever believe?" She shakes her head. "The woman is Chinese, for goodness sake, but Wei's parents claimed she's too westernized and doesn't understand Wei's culture. It got pretty ugly, and eventually, she had to let it go. You should still take him," she says, sensing my determination wavering. "You have to report it."

"Okay." I nod, feeling unsure and in way over my head.

She claps her hands, and every child in her classroom sits up straight in their chair and waits for her instruction. "Follow me, children, we're going to be visiting Miss Holland's classroom. Single file, please, and no running in the corridor." They do exactly as they've been told, shuffling past us in neat, orderly lines.

"How do you do that?" I whisper.

"Years of practice," she whispers back.

BIANCA'S OFFICE door is closed, but the bright-eyed secretary outside it lets her know that we're here to see her and promises she will only be a few minutes.

"Miss Holland?" Bianca gives me a curious smile as soon as she opens her door, which falters as her eyes fall on Wei.

"I'm so sorry to bother you. I know you said you had meetings today, but we had an incident in class."

"Well, in that case, you better come in. Wei, you wait here with Miss Candice, I'll call for you when we're ready."

Wei simply slouches deeper in his chair.

Bianca's office is a safe haven for parents. Every detail, from the pale cream upholstered sofa to the dozens of framed photographs of past students adorning the walls, makes you feel as if you could tell her anything.

She gets straight to the point. "What happened?"

I tell her, trying to narrate the incident from an objective point of view. When I'm done, Bianca presses her fingertips to her temples.

"This isn't the first time this has happened, I'm afraid. I feel bad that you're the one having to deal with him, being so newly employed, but he was placed in that class at the beginning of the academic year and I didn't want to move him. He doesn't cope well with change."

"It's fine, I can handle it," I insist. "If you could just tell me *how* to handle it."

She smiles. "Wei is a very difficult case. His parents are, unfortunately, almost impossible to get hold of, and, when we do manage to get them here long enough to discuss anything, they simply deny that their child is the problem." She gets to her feet and riffles through an orderly filing cabinet behind her desk. "Here," she says, handing me a hefty Manila folder. "This is Wei's file. You should read through it, so you know what you're dealing with. It's quite a tome," she adds, apologetically, "it might take you a while. If, after a few weeks, you feel you can't handle him, I'll re-allocate him to a different teacher." I can tell that she really, really doesn't want to do that, and I suspect it's because of how Wei's parents would react. Silently, I vow that I won't complain, no matter how bad things get. Bianca gave me a chance, despite my lack of experience. I'm not about to let her down, not if I can help it.

"What do we do now, though?" I ask.

"We call him in and explain again that there are rules to be followed. It's about all we can do at this point. We'll also have to let the parents of the other children involved know what happened – you'll find their email addresses in your class register. You mentioned Gabby was one of the children who was hurt?"

"Yes."

She grimaces. "Gabby's mom isn't exactly a walk in the park. Let me know how she responds. If need be, I'll get hold of her myself."

"I'm sure it'll be fine," I say, my fake confidence improving in leaps and bounds.

"Thank you," Bianca says, and she sounds like she means it.

"I BET you could use a stiff drink about now," Mandy says when I catch up to her and Kate at the front gate after the final bell.

"You have no idea," I say, automatically. In truth, I could go home and sleep for days. "Are kids always this exhausting?"

"Every. Single. Day." Each word is a sentence on its own as she drives her point home.

"Don't scare her off," Kate warns, "we can't afford another Fenn."

"Who's Fenn?" I ask as I fall into step between them.

"She's the teacher you replaced," Mandy says. "She said she was going back to South Africa, but we're pretty sure she had a nervous breakdown. Kate swears she saw her waiting tables in a pub downtown."

I look to Kate for confirmation, and she nods sagely in agreement.

"I'm too young for a breakdown." I grin. "I've got my whole life ahead of me."

"Miss Amber!" The sound of Denri's horn almost sends all three of us off the sidewalk and into the bushes beyond.

"Denri!" I squawk, my hand clapped to my chest. With everything that had happened today, I'd completely forgotten to let him know not to fetch me. I hurry to the car, idling beside us. "I'm so sorry, I forgot to text you. I'm going for a drink with my friends." I gesture at Mandy and Kate and Denri waves enthusiastically.

"You go drinky drinky?"

"Yes," I laugh, "we go drinky drinky."

"In, in. I give you lift!"

I feel too bad to decline, given that he's come out especially for me. We pile into the Volkswagen, Mandy grumbling that it's only a minute away, and Denri whips away from the sidewalk, redlining the little engine in first gear.

We take a left turn, hit second gear, and Mandy yells for him to stop.

"We're here," she explains, pointing at a low-roofed building on our left and I burst out laughing.

AT FIRST GLANCE, I gather that what Mandy deems to be amazing, and what I deem to be amazing are two very different things. *Calico's* is a grimy little pub with bad lighting and stale peanuts. Then I discover that cocktails are half-price on a Monday night, and I find the appeal. A teaching salary and an entertainment budget are not synonymous. I'd offered for Denri to join us, but he'd driven off quite happily, promising that he'd pick me up for work in the morning. He'd even gone as far as to say he'd collect me when I was done having 'drinky drinkys', but I'd told him I was perfectly capable of catching a bus. Or a taxi. It turns out Kate lives only a few streets down from me, so at least there's no chance I'll get lost.

Armed with Mojitos and a bowl of salted peanuts, we navigate our way to an empty table. It takes about twenty minutes, as Mandy stops to say hi to almost every person in the pub.

"You come here often?" I tease, as we finally take our seats.

"What can I say, I'm a friendly girl."

"Mandy knows everyone," Kate interjects. "You'll get used to it."

"A toast," Mandy announces, raising her glass, "To Amber's first day."

"To Amber's first day," Kate echoes.

"To you two," I interject, "for helping me get through it."

"So, Amber," Mandy says after downing half her Mojito in one impressive gulp. "What's your story?"

"My story?"

"Yes, your story." She rolls her eyes. "Amber Holland in thirty seconds or less. Why are you here, where have you been? Are you single, married, divorced? Straight, gay, bi? The possibilities are endless."

"Okay." I've never been one to back down from a challenge. "It's probably easier to tell you where I haven't been – Australia springs to mind, actually." I frown, ticking her questions off one by one. "Single. Definitely single. And straight – although there was this one time at college that I seriously considered the alternative. As to why I'm here, we're going to need another drink, and a hell of a lot longer than thirty seconds."

Mandy grins and raises her hand to flag the nearest waiter. "Challenge accepted," she says.

It takes two cocktails and almost an hour before I'm done talking.

"Holy shiiiiit," Mandy drawls, after a long silence. "You really are a poor little rich girl." I'm fast learning that one of Mandy's many charms is the ability to turn an insult into an endearment.

"I am," I say, dropping my head.

"Look, to be fair, it sounds as though you might've needed an intervention. Not that it doesn't suck," she adds graciously, "but it'll probably do you the world of good."

"I can't argue with that."

"You mean you wouldn't dare," Kate teases. Her eyes are sparkling, and her cheeks are flushed. Now that I think about it, I'm feeling quite tipsy myself. I order a sparkling water and, to my relief, neither of them passes comment.

"Enough about me. I want to hear your stories."

Kate goes first.

"I'm engaged." She holds up her hand, and I notice for the first time the delicate diamond ring on her finger. "My fiancé, Tim, is flying out to visit the week after next."

"He's still in England?"

"Yeah. He'd just started a new job in banking, something he's been wanting for ages, when I was offered this post."

"Kate has only white picket fences in her future, and she won't admit it, but she's already named all three of her children," Mandy says, with absolutely no underlying judgment and a heavy trace of admiration in her voice.

"Oh, shut it, you."

"How long have you and Tim been together?" I ask.

She blushes. "Ten years, since I was fourteen."

"Childhood sweethearts," Mandy says. "It's so sweet it hurts my teeth."

"That is seriously impressive," I say. "Do I get to meet him? When he comes over, I mean?"

"Of course!"

"Have you met him?" I ask Mandy.

"No, but I've witnessed enough of their video calls to know that he's perfect for our Kate."

"Isn't it hard being apart?" I ask.

Kate twists her engagement ring around her finger. "Very. Tim had been retrenched when we started the process to come over here, but then he got this other offer, which was too good to refuse, and plans changed. I'm going to stick it out for the year. I think it's been good for us. We've never been apart, so I see it as a true test of our relationship."

I meet Mandy's eyes, and she gives me a pointed look. "What did I tell you? Adorable."

"What about you?" I ask her. "Is there a handsome Aussie waiting for you back home?"

She looks horror-struck. "Hell no! Treat 'em mean, keep 'em clean and all that. Besides, I'm far too indecisive to be stuck with one guy. No offense, Kate."

"None taken."

Mandy waves her hand in a lazy circle. "The world is too big, and men are far too interesting to commit to just one."

BY THE TIME our shared cab drops me outside my apartment building, I'm well and truly ready for bed, but I force myself to open Wei's file. It's exactly as I suspected – endless reports of anti-social behavior, rule-breaking, bullying. He's bright though, well above his grade average. This kid is going to be a serious problem, is my last conscious thought before I collapse face first on my pillow.

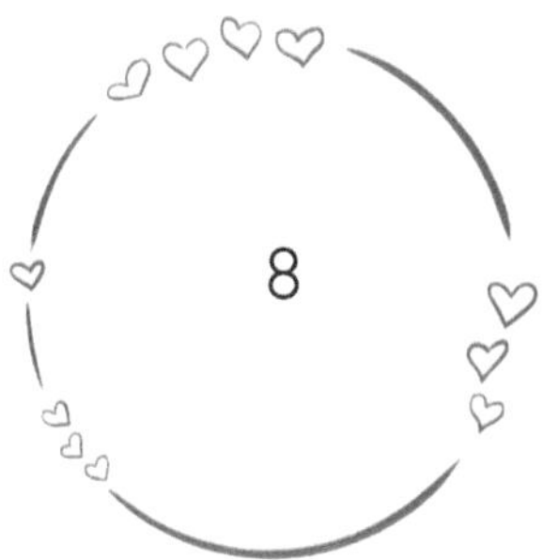

8

Gabby Martin's mother blows into my classroom the following morning like a hurricane intent on vengeance.

"I want that boy expelled!" she roars, pointing a red-taloned finger at Wei. Her plump face is contorted in an ugly scowl, her flabby upper arm exposed and quivering as her shirt sleeve hitches up.

"Mrs. Martin!" I exclaim, shocked to my core. "Can we speak outside, please? This is not the time, or the place to discuss this."

"You're the new one?"

"I am yes. I'm Gabby's new teacher, Amber Holland." I extend my hand, and she blatantly ignores it. Her icy blue eyes narrow beneath her platinum fringe as she takes me in.

"Exactly how new? When did you graduate?"

"I..." Caught off guard, it takes me a moment to find my words. "I don't think that has anything to do with the issue at hand."

"When *my* daughter comes home covered in bruises after being in *your* care and all I get is an unsatisfactory email in explanation, I think I have the right to voice my concerns."

I'm hyper aware that every one of my students has frozen in their tracks, listening to every word. Wei has gone rigid, his entire body tensed. Even Gabby looks miserable, head hanging at her mother's side.

"That may well be, but I am not discussing this in front of the children."

She relents and follows me outside into the hall. Before I step out of the classroom, I give Wei an encouraging smile, and I'm astonished to find he's close to tears.

I don't give Gabby's mom the opportunity to build up any more steam.

"Mrs. Martin, I understand that you're upset, but I have the situation under control. Both myself and Principal Chen have spoken to Wei and I'm keeping a strict eye on him. I do think," I add, knowing that this isn't going to go down well, "that he has some issues at home, and I think we need to keep in mind that sometimes children lash out when they are under emotional strain."

"If he's mentally unsound, that's even more reason he shouldn't be in a classroom with normal children." This woman's capacity for compassion is non-existent. I take a deep breath.

"Mrs. Martin, before the incident where Gabby got hurt occurred, I witnessed her pinching Wei. It was earlier in the day, and she did it without any provocation."

Shonda Martin may be blonde, but she isn't stupid. The second the full implication of my words hit home, her brows shoot up, and her shoulders go rigid.

"Are you trying to imply that my child is responsible for what happened?"

"I'm not implying anything, I'm simply giving you the bigger picture," I say quickly. My brain is whirring, trying to find the right words to appease this woman without insulting her. I dig deep and channel every ounce of my father's diplomacy. "I don't think we should overreact just yet. I'm new to this classroom, and I don't know the children well enough to have an informed opinion, but I can promise you that I won't tolerate bullying, Gabby is in good hands." I can't believe how easily that came out of my mouth. Oh my God, I almost sounded like a real teacher. If only Kent and my dad could see me now, I think, beaming with pride.

My moment of triumph lasts about two point seven seconds.

"Do you find this amusing?"

I snap back to reality to find Shonda Martin glaring at me.

"No, of course I don't." *Please just let it go, please just let it go*

"I want to speak to Principal Chen."

Shit.

I gather myself and give her a brief nod of understanding. "I can arrange that."

"Don't you dare! You're not to leave my child unattended with that boy. I know where her office is, I'll see myself over there."

"I hope you trip," I growl under my breath as she clacks off in her high heels. Then I paste a smile on my face and head back into my classroom.

FORTUNATELY, nothing comes of Shonda's visit. Bianca sends me a brief email to say that it's all sorted and that I handled it perfectly. I reply with an apology that it had to be escalated to her, but that I am keeping a strict eye on Wei.

By the second week of school, I've tentatively adjusted, and more or less found a routine. I wake up, go for a quick run to a coffee shop two blocks down, where I reward my efforts with a small vanilla latte. I take a far more leisurely walk back, shower, and slurp down a peanut butter and banana smoothie while I wait for Denri. I told him that I'm more than capable of finding my own way to work, but he insists that the school is on his way and he doesn't mind at all. Well, at least that what I think he said. With Denri, it's hard to be sure. He looks happy about it, though.

Week two goes by with no incidents. Wei is sullen but keeping mostly to himself. I find it hard to believe that Gabby's mom frightened him enough to curb his bad behavior, and in my more optimistic moods, I wonder if he feels bad that he got me into trouble. I've treated him with nothing but kindness and encouragement, and I've praised his work wherever possible. Still, he is a closed book. I try to talk to Kate and Mandy about it during our daily lunches, but Mandy shoots me down, and Kate has no words of wisdom to impart. Friday arrives faster than I anticipated, and despite it being an uneventful week, I'm exhausted.

I'm packing up after school, dreaming of a good movie – even if it does have subtitles – and a hot bath, when Mandy bursts into my classroom, Kate right behind her.

"Amber, do you know what rhymes with Friday?"

"Duvet?"

"No." She lifts her hands theatrically. "Champagne."

"That doesn't rhyme at all." I stack the last of the chairs so the cleaners won't bitch and moan – a lesson I learned after last weekend, and catch Kate's eye. She winks. "I'm beat," I tell Mandy half-heartedly.

"Shake your ass, we're going to my place," she says as if I haven't spoken.

"Is it worth arguing?" I ask Kate.

"Not even a little bit," she replies.

"YOU LIVE HERE?" I can't keep the disbelief from my voice as I gaze up at the palatial apartment block.

"I do. And don't look at me like that, Miss *Thang*. From what you've told us about your life back in the States, you should feel right at home." Mandy breezes saunters inside. and we follow her into an exquisite foyer, complete with gleaming marble floors and fresh flowers on every surface.

The elevator hisses open, and Mandy jabs the button for the 15th floor. The *top* floor.

"You live in the penthouse?" I'm still slack-jawed, and Kate stifles a giggle. "What are you not telling me?"

"If I told you, I'd have to kill you," Mandy replies, non-committal.

My entire apartment could fit into Mandy's cream and gold living room. The west wall is comprised of enormous concertina glass doors which open onto a wide balcony. I catch a glimpse of a hot tub – a hot tub! – and two pool loungers, but before I can look any further, we've passed into the kitchen. It's monochrome heaven – stark black and white broken only by the sleek silver of top-end appliances. Black lamp shades hang above the vast white Caesarstone island in the center. I rotate on the spot, taking it all in, and then I round on Mandy, who is rummaging in the fridge.

"Is there something you want to tell me, Mandy?" I ask, and then when she glances over her shoulder to look at me, "the name of your sugar daddy, perhaps?"

"Actually, I'm just a responsible adult who manages her finances well." She grins before turning back to the contents of the fridge. She retrieves a chilled bottle of champagne and starts to open it. Kate has already fetched three glasses from a cupboard on the opposite side of the island.

The cork pops, missing my head by less than an inch.

"You're seriously not going to explain all of this?" I ask, raising a brow.

She only hands me a glass and wags her finger at me. "Drink up."

"A toast," Kate says, "to Friday."

"Which rhymes with champagne," I add, and we clink glasses. I take a long sip and then give a sigh of pleasure. "Man, that tastes good."

Kate, I notice, has downed half her glass in a single swig.

"Rough week, Kate?" I ask

She shakes her head, wiping champagne from the corners of her mouth. "I just really enjoy champagne. Especially the expensive kind."

"You can see why we became friends," Mandy says.

To my delight, we head for the balcony. Mandy and I sink onto the loungers, while Kate takes a seat on the edge of the hot tub, her feet in the water.

"It's like a free massage," she explains, moving her foot over the jets.

"I'm never leaving this spot," I tell them, closing my eyes and feeling the late afternoon sun on my face.

Mandy tops up my glass. "Don't you dare fall asleep. I'm not carrying you back inside."

"When does Tim arrive?" I ask Kate.

"Next Friday." Her voice is honey and light. It's the same voice she always uses when she talks about Tim.

"How long is he here for?"

"Only a week. He can't get any more time off work."

You must be so excited."

"I am. And I can't wait for you guys to meet him."

"Never ever have I ever met Kate's fiancé," Mandy drawls. Kate tips her glass and drinks.

"You know that game?" I adore it. Lara and I used to play it all the time.

"Never ever have I ever played never ever have I ever," Mandy says in response, and we all drink.

When the sky darkens and the night air begins to chill, we move inside. Mandy sits on the floor, on a soft cream rug, while Kate and I take opposite ends of the sofa.

"Never have I ever been caught doing it by my parents," Mandy says. We both take a sip of our champagne, but Kate remains still.

"Seriously, Kate? Your parents must be blinded by that halo floating above your head," I say.

"Never ever have I sexted," Mandy prompts, giving Kate a knowing grin. When she raises her glass, Mandy laughs and offers her the bottle. "You may as well drink it all."

Kate takes it. "Well, I am in a long-distance relationship."

. . .

WHEN I DISCOVER that Mandy has Netflix, I call the game to a halt.

"No subtitles!" I shriek, bouncing on the couch like a schoolgirl.

"You don't have Netflix?" They're both horrified.

"Cut off, remember?" I say, making scissor movements with my free hand.

"You can log into my account," Mandy offers. I give her my phone, and she sets it up. Seeing the familiar icon on my screen brings me insurmountable joy. I'm still staring at it when a text comes through from Kent. *How's employed life? You hanging in there?*

I squint at the screen through champagne goggles and send a reply: *Better than hanging in, I've even made friends.*

"I need a selfie," I announce. "Mandy, get up here."

She grumbles but gets off the floor to join us on the couch.

"Who are you sending it to?" she asks, once I've snapped six photos - three were blurred, and Kate had her eyes closed in two.

"Kent," I say automatically, forwarding the photo. I can see that he's typing, so I stare at the screen, oblivious to the fact that they've fallen silent.

That looks like trouble with a capital T ;)

I'm so stunned he's used the wink emoji that I drop my phone to find Mandy and Kate staring at me.

"What?"

"Who," Mandy begins.

"Is," Kate adds.

"Kent?" Combined, their voices are amplified.

"Did you guys plan that?"

My phone pings again, but before I can reach for it, Mandy snatches it up.

"I'm glad you're having fun," she reads aloud. Her fingers tap the screen in rapid succession, and then she zooms in. "Holy shit! Who *is* he?" she swings the phone around so the screen is in my face. Kent's profile picture fills my vision. It's a good picture. He's even almost smiling.

"Kent," I say, confusion setting in. *Surely I've told them about Kent?*

Kate leans into my shoulder to get a better look. "Woah!"

I groan. It's easy to forget how attractive women find the bastard.

"If this is what California men look like, I'm booking the next flight out," Mandy says.

"Stop it," I snap, grabbing my phone. "Trust me when I say, it'd be a waste of money. Although," I add, giving Mandy a wry look, "apparently you can afford it."

"Nice try," she says, reaching for the open bottle on the table and pausing the movie. "But I'm not pressing tit until you spill the beans."

"Honestly, there's nothing to tell. He's an old friend. A very old friend. As in, we used to swim naked in the pool together old."

"Kinky bitch."

"Very funny. But seriously, you guys, it's not like that. So, can we please get back to the lovely, no subtitles, movie?"

"He sent you a wink emoji," Mandy says as if that settles the matter.

I frown. That *was* weird. Kent doesn't use emojis, certainly not with me, anyway. I pick up my phone to check. It's definitely a wink. Still, I scroll up to show them our entire thread, which is a few short lines.

"See?" I say. "It's nothing."

Mandy actually puts her finger to my screen, as if calling my bluff, to see if there's more. When she discovers there's not, her face falls.

"What a waste."

"Not really. He's nice to look at, but he's a pain in the ass. You wouldn't like him."

"Methinks the girl doth protest too much," Kate says, and then lets out a spectacular burp.

I wake with a crick in my neck and a Kate-sized hot water bottle curled into my back. I blink a few times, testing my head, but I feel fine. After two bottles of champagne, Mandy had made a pot of coffee, and we'd stayed up later than we should have, but all in all, it really was just an innocent girls' night in. I can't remember the last time I did that. Lara would rather have been burned at the stake than admit to spending an evening at home. My lips curve upward as a rare sense of pride rises in my chest.

"Please don't tell me you're a morning person." Mandy hands me an enormous mug, steaming caffeine fumes. "The sun's barely up, and you look far too happy for my liking."

"*You're* up," I point out, carefully extracting myself from Kate, who is snoring softly.

"I forgot to close my curtains," she says, "the sun almost singed my eyelids."

Not even the heavenly smell of coffee can rouse Kate. "Should we wake her?" I ask, jabbing her with my toe when the snoring stops, to see if she's still breathing.

Mandy grins. "I have a better idea."

Kate wakes as we're applying the finishing touches to her face.

"You are both assholes," Kate groans five minutes later as she surveys the damage in the bathroom mirror. "And how do you even own a lipstick that red?" she demands.

"That wasn't mine," Mandy admits. "That was all Amber."

Kate wipes futilely at her clown-painted face.

"It's a stay-on," I manage, through peals of laughter. "Twenty-four hours of Moulin *Rouge*, or your money back. But look on the bright side. By this time tomorrow, you'll be fine."

"I am not leaving this apartment until it's off!"

Mandy catches my eye and shrugs. "I guess we'll have to watch a shit-ton of non-subtitled movies."

I GET HOME in the early afternoon. It turns out even expensive stay-on lipstick is no match for MAC Pro make-up remover, so Kate left at the same time. Mandy has plans for this evening, though she refused to tell us what they were, or, more importantly, with whom.

After a quick shower, during which I lament the fact that I keep bumping my elbows on the tiled wall while washing my hair, especially after the luxury of Mandy's double-wide, I settle on the sofa in a t-shirt and shorts, with a towel wrapped around my wet hair, and a cucumber sandwich which, thanks to Kate, is my new favorite thing.

I've just taken a bite when my phone beeps.

I hope your evening ended well?

The sandwich loses all appeal. It's not hard to read between the lines. Kent wants to know if I got out of hand last night. I reply with another selfie we'd taken shortly before bed, coffee cups on clear display, and the caption: *Wild Night*. Now that I look at it, I notice Kate's eyes are closed again.

No getting lost, then?

I don't dignify that with a response, and his next text comes through a few seconds later.

I'm flying in on Tuesday. Dinner Wednesday night?

I'll have to check my schedule. Oh, screw it. Who am I trying to fool? *You better be paying.*

Saber can pay ;) That damn emoji again! *I'll pick you up at 7.*

I reply with a champagne emoji, just to piss him off, but he doesn't check his phone again.

ON MONDAY MORNING, I find Mandy in the staff room with the biggest pair of sunglasses I have ever seen perched on her face. She's clutching a steaming mug of coffee as if her life depends on it.

"Rough night?" I ask primly as if I haven't been in her situation a thousand times before.

"I feel like I've been hit by a 10-tonne truck. Please tell me I at least look a little better than I feel?"

"All I can see are those glasses. Are those Prada?" I add, catching sight of the familiar logo. "Honestly, girl, you have got to let me in on whatever, or whoever, it is you're up to. Or at least introduce me to his brother."

Kate breezes in, a veritable ray of sunshine. "Morning! Ooh, I like your dress, Amber."

"Thanks." I smooth down the bright floral skirt. "I had a productive afternoon yesterday. I found an absolute gem of a market, only a few blocks down from my apartment." I'd been thrilled to discover it was cheap as chips, too, but I don't mention that.

"It hurts my eyes," Mandy groans, but she reaches out and rubs the fabric between her fingers. "Very pretty, though. Your legs look fantastic."

Kate frowns, noticing Mandy's glasses. "Are you okay?"

"No. I'm dying."

"We have a fire drill in twenty minutes," Kate warns. "I heard Bianca telling maintenance on my way over here."

"This is going to be the longest day ever. I didn't get a wink of sleep last night. I don't know how much longer I can carry on doing this without keeling over."

"Doing what?" I ask, pouncing on her moment of weakness.

She feigns ignorance, but not before I catch the flash of guilt on her face. "Just balancing my busy social life and this lousy paying job."

I open my mouth to tell her she needs to spend a few nights at home, catching up on sleep, realize it's exactly what Kent would say, and shut it.

"I hope the kids take it easy on you today," I say instead.

"I'd never get that lucky," she moans. "If I go missing, don't forget to check under my desk in case I've passed out underneath it."

THE CHILDREN ARE impossible after the fire drill. In an effort to calm them down, I read a storybook – *Three Billy Goats Gruff*, and then I allocate them an independent task, to write their own fairy tale, my only requirement that it be at least a full page long. That should keep them quiet for at least half an hour. I sit at my desk, surreptitiously watching Wei. To my surprise, he barely lifts his head from the page, his face close to the paper, tongue sticking out between his teeth in concentration.

I collect every paper before the lunch bell rings and, on impulse, shove them into my bag before dismissing the children.

To my surprise, Kate is alone at our usual table.

"Where is she?" I ask, peering around trying to spot Mandy.

"She's not here. She went home. Stomach flu, apparently," she adds loudly, as one of the other teachers passes close to our table.

"Do you know?" I ask Kate the second he's gone. "Where she gets the money?"

Kate gives me a long look. "No," she admits finally.

"You haven't asked?"

"It's none of my business. If she wanted us to know, we'd know."

Sensing she doesn't want to discuss it, I change the topic by asking about Tim. I've already learned that nothing perks Kate up quite like the mention of her man.

Before the next class starts, I send a quick text to Mandy: *All ok?* And then I hurry into my classroom and put my phone in my desk drawer. I whip it out the second the children have filed out at the end of the school day and am relieved to see she's replied.

All good, just feeling shite! I blame no sleep and bad sushi.

That brings a smile to my lips. Bad sushi – even I've used that one. Mandy and I are far more alike than she believes. I hastily type out a response. *Let me know if you need me to bring you anything. Hope you feel better x*

My phone pings almost immediately. *I should be good by morning, thanks x*

I READ through the children's stories with the TV on low in the background and a bowl of stir-fried vegetable perched on my knees. The stories are sweet – utter plagiarism and peppered with 'and thens', but all in all, I'm proud of the work they've put in. I save Wei's until last. I have no idea what it is about him that intrigues me so much, but he's like an enigma I need to solve. His behavior since the incident has improved, but I've noticed he hardly ever interacts with any of the other children anymore.

The forkful of food goes cold halfway to my lips as I read Wei's piece. Then I drop it back into the bowl and read it again.

Wei's story is simple. He's retold the story of the three billy goats, but he's done something remarkable – something I'd never have expected a seven-year-old mind to consider. He's told it from the troll's point of view.

I snatch up my phone and call Kate.

"Hey!" I say, the second she answers. "Sorry to call so late, you weren't sleeping, were you?"

"No, not at all," she says, in the high-pitched tone that someone adopts when they're trying desperately to sound like they haven't just woken up.

"I'm sorry, I just had to talk to someone about this. Have you ever taught Wei?"

"Wei Li?"

"Yes. Have you ever taught him?"

"No, why?"

"He's a genius. I mean, I think he might be really gifted. I set the kids a task today, to write me a story. I read *Three Billy Goats Gruff* to them first, as an example, and they were all pretty much the same thing – rehashing of common fairy tales. But his story was... hang on, let me read it to you."

"Wow," she says when I'm done.

"I know, right? And he's only seven!"

"That really is brilliant," she murmurs, sounding lost in thought.

"It's genius! And his writing – spelling, grammar, punctuation – it's incredible, especially seeing that it's not his first language."

"What are you going to do about it?"

"Besides give him a big fat A? I'm going to speak to Bianca. I told you I majored in English literature, right?" I don't wait for her confirmation, "well, anyway, I took a bunch of creative writing courses on the side, and I really think this kid has serious talent. Who knows, he might even find it a creative outlet for all that pent-up anger he's holding on to."

Kate is silent a long moment. When she speaks again, her voice is gentle. "Are you sure you're not blowing this out of proportion? I know you've got a soft spot for him."

That takes me by surprise. "No, I don't."

Her soft laughter tinkles through the phone. "Amber, Wei has been in trouble more times than I can count. Not a week goes by at school that someone isn't lodging a complaint about him, but other than that first day, you haven't spoken a bad word about him. Teachers bitch," she adds, "it's what we do."

"I'm not really a teacher," I remind her. "I don't know how it works."

"Bullshit. You're a fantastic teacher. You even have a soft spot for the troubled ones."

I THINK LONG and hard after we hang up. I can't deny that when Kate had called me a fantastic teacher, I'd felt a surge of pride so intense it made my chest hurt. I've only been doing this job a few weeks, but I already feel like it's what I was meant to do. For the first time in my life, I have a sense of purpose, and a feeling of complete responsibility. These twelve children are on my watch, and I find, to my utmost surprise, that I really don't want to let the little shits down.

I'm in such a euphoric mood that when Kent texts me in the middle of the night, oblivious or uncaring of the time difference, to confirm dinner on Wednesday night, and instructing me to dress up, not down, I send him a hug emoji without even thinking.

10

Mandy is back at work the following morning, looking more like her old self, if a little pale. Her sandy hair is pulled back into a messy bun, but her hazel eyes are on full display - no dark glasses in sight.

"I swear I've lost about five pounds," she tells us, looking thrilled.

"And all of it ego," Kate teases.

"I'm glad you're feeling better," I say, glancing at my watch. "I've got to run, I want to catch Bianca before the bell. We'll catch up at lunch?"

"Why are you going to the principal's office?" Mandy asks. "Did I miss something? Did something happen?"

"Nothing to worry about," I say, already halfway out the door. "Kate can fill you in. See you later!"

BIANCA IS SITTING at her desk, intent on her computer. When she spots me over the top of the screen, she waves me in.

"Amber! What brings you to my door so early?"

"I wanted to catch you before class," I explain, hurrying over to sit opposite her. "It's about Wei Li."

Her face falls. "Please don't tell me I'll be dealing with Shonda Martin today. I'm neck-deep in budget reviews, and I don't think I have the energy."

"No," I smile. "There will be zero difficult parents on the agenda today. In fact, this is *good* news." I slide Wei's story across the desk toward her. She arches a perfect black brow.

"I don't think I've ever heard the words 'Wei' and 'good' mentioned in a single conversation before." She picks up the sheet of paper. "What am I looking at?"

"It's a task I set for the children yesterday. I asked them to write a fairy tale, after reading one to them."

"Nice," she murmurs approvingly, while her eyes scan the page. She's referring to the task, not Wei's work.

"Thanks," I murmur, and then I hold my breath. Bianca's reaction is not quite as enthusiastic as mine, had been, but her lips curve upward as she scans the page again.

"He's a very smart little boy," she finally acknowledges, passing it back to me. I feel oddly deflated. It's a positive response, but not the one I was expecting. I try to remember that Bianca's been doing this a lot longer than I have, she's probably seen her share of talent over the years.

"It's fantastic," I say, my confidence draining by the second.

"Indeed. What I'm wondering though, is why you've brought it to me?"

"I..." I trail off, not sure what to say.

"You can speak freely, Amber."

"Well, it's just that he's obviously talented, and I think with a bit of encouragement and some work, he could really excel in class – not just at English, but in general."

Now her smile blazes.

"What?" I ask.

"I'm impressed. I knew Wei was something special within a week of him starting here, but unfortunately, as principal, there wasn't much I could do about it. Not without a teacher who was prepared to invest in him. And, as I'm sure you know, none have been particularly fond of the boy. I have been waiting for two years for someone to recognize his potential. The question is, what are *you* going to do about it?"

"I was kind of hoping you'd tell me."

She smiles, leans forward over her desk and clasps her hands together.

"If you're up to it, I'd like to speak to his parents about private tutoring. Possibly enrolling him in a new school – one for children who might match his intellectual level. Wei needs to be challenged," she adds quickly, catching sight of my crestfallen face. "There is no doubt that he's a bright boy, but if I were to hazard a guess, he is also borderline autistic. Being bored and completely understimulated isn't a healthy environment, but unfortunately, his parents refuse to acknowledge it."

"You want me to encourage them to move him?"

"Right now, I just want you to give him something he hasn't had before. A chance."

"If I agree," I say slowly, my mind racing, "would his parents even consent to me working privately with him?"

"It would mean his school hours would be extended, twice a week. Yours too," she adds, almost as an afterthought. "It would mean less time they'd have to worry about actually parenting. I'm quite certain they wouldn't have an issue with it." Her tone is acid, and for the first time, I catch a glimpse of just how much she dislikes Wei's parents.

"Ultimately, though, you want him to move schools?"

She smiles at that. "I don't want Wei moved because he's a nuisance," she says firmly. "I want him moved because it would be the best thing for him. Quite frankly, he deserves better."

. . .

BY WEDNESDAY AFTERNOON, Bianca still hasn't confirmed whether Wei's parents have agreed to extra tutoring or not, and I'm grateful for the distraction of dinner with Kent. I'm also absurdly excited to see him. I may be settling in well to my new life, but that doesn't mean that I don't miss home. I'd prefer my mom, but in her absence, I'm quite happy to take Kent instead. I'm also not so changed that I'm not thrilled at the prospect of dressing up.

I rummage through my closet, ignoring the more conservative outfits that have come to the fore as suitable work attire, and pull out one of my staple favorites – a simple, fitting black dress with a neckline high enough for anyone born after 1960, and low enough that Kent is bound to disapprove. I slip on a pair of strappy black heels, which were once my favorite pair, and find them oddly uncomfortable. At least my legs look good, thanks to weeks of running, and living off rice and vegetables. My mouth salivates at the thought of a rare steak dripping in garlic butter.

By six, I'm dressed and ready, with an hour to spare, so I send Kent a text to tell him I'll meet him at his hotel. Of course, he's 5-star accommodated over at *The Ritz-Carlton.*

THE CAB RIDE is only a few minutes, but as early as I am, I still find Kent waiting at the downstairs bar, his broad-shouldered back to me.

"I hope I'm at least getting a bottle of Moët for putting on these heels," I tease before he sees me.

"I thought you preferred tequila straight from the bottle," he replies easily as he turns around. His eyes drop to my chest, then keep going, taking in every inch of the dress before they rise to meet mine. His lips twitch upward in approval. "You look good." He puts a warm hand to my cheek and brushes his thumb below my eye. "The shadows are gone. You must be getting more sleep these days." The gesture is platonic, but it leaves a trail of fire across my cheek.

"I'm the poster girl for morals and virtue," I say, trying to keep my tone light as I duck away from his hand.

"No Moët," he says, turning back to the bar. "The last time we drank it together, you broke three bones."

IN OUR SENIOR year of high school, unbeknownst to my parents who had taken a short trip abroad, Kent and I had successfully pulled off the party of the summer. We'd managed to smuggle in copious amounts of alcohol, mostly beer, but Kent had (and I'm still not sure how he did it) managed to secure four bottles of Moët & Chandon. We'd shared the beer. The champagne, we'd kept to ourselves.

By the end of the night, I was dancing on the table, barefoot, with Kent on the floor beside me, mimicking my moves. I still don't know how I slipped, but I'd ended up in a heap on the floor. Mortified, I'd stumbled to my feet, only to find, as I attempted a dignified walk away, I couldn't put an ounce of weight on my left foot.

"It's fine, it's only a sprain," I'd argued when Kent insisted on taking me to the emergency room. Two days later, the swelling had reached epic proportions, and the pain was so bad I could barely move my leg without crying out. Kent had bravely confided in his mother, and Janine had taken the two of us to the hospital, with a dire warning that my parents would be hearing about the party. The X-rays showed I'd broken three bones.

I'd been on crutches for twelve weeks. Worse, the boot I'd had to wear resulted in the most horrendous suntan, which Kent had ridiculed the rest of the summer.

"WHERE DID YOU GET THAT MOËT?" I ask him now. He'd never told me.

"I bought it. Well, I got Alan Kirby's older brother to buy it. I blew my entire savings on that champagne."

"Why? We had enough beer that night to start our own pub."

He shrugs. "You said you'd always wanted to try it."

I lift my head in surprise.

"What, you don't remember?"

"I do. It's just... well, it's hard to remember that you used to do things like that for me. We're so different now."

"We grew up."

I throw him a wry look. "Well, you did."

"You look pretty grown up right now," he says, and then a devilish glint comes into his eyes. "Ah, screw it. Let's get the Moët."

"Kent James! I'm shocked. Look at you, living on the edge."

Kent orders a bottle to be sent to our table and we make our way through the crowded restaurant to be seated.

"What are you going to do if I break a bone?" I ask as the waiter pours us each a glass. It's ice cold and delicious, and the bubbles tickle my nose when I take my first sip.

"I'll drive you to the emergency room. I won't even need to call my mom in for back-up."

"*So* grown up." I laugh.

Kent picks up his menu. "What are you having?"

"Steak. Definitely steak."

"I'll have the same." He closes his menu with a snap, and the waiter appears as if by magic to take our order.

"Tell me about your job. How are you enjoying teaching?"

I tell him about Mandy and Kate, and the children in my class. When I get to Wei, I'm so caught up in the topic that I speak, non-stop, for a good ten minutes. Kent doesn't interrupt me once. He only refills my glass and waves the waiter away when he approaches to check on us.

"Why are you looking at me like that?" I ask when, at long last, I run out of steam.

"I'm a little stunned, actually. It sounds like you're *actually* enjoying yourself. And given that you're having fun which doesn't include partying all night and sleeping all day, you're going to have to give me a minute to process."

"Shut up."

"I'm not insulting you, Amber. I'm proud of you."

"I'm actually quite proud of myself."

"Are you really going to tutor Wei? If his parents agree, I mean?"

I nod. "I'd like to. He's a special kid."

"He's lucky to have you."

"That's the third compliment you've given me this evening. Be careful, it might even become a habit."

"I have no problem giving praise where it's due."

"Ouch." My light-hearted mood deflates slightly. It's a stinging reminder that he hasn't had much to praise me for in a while. Before either of us can say anything else, the food arrives.

"Why are you spending so much time in Beijing?" I ask, the second the waiter departs. If Kent knows I'm trying to change the subject, he doesn't argue.

"We just closed a major development deal. I'm back in four weeks, and I'll be staying a while. At least until all the preliminary work is finalized."

"You're going to be staying here? In Beijing?"

He chuckles, low and melodious. "Do you have a problem with that?"

"No, actually. It'll be nice to have a familiar face around."

His brows arch. "You expect me to believe that Amber Holland might find my company tolerable?"

"Well," I tease, holding up my glass, "you do have your charms."

"It's nice to see that you haven't completely transformed. I thought I might have to book you into a convent."

"I'm still me. I may have taken things a bit too far for a while, but I was never exactly convent material."

"No arguments there," he concedes, clinking his glass against mine.

. . .

WE ONLY HAVE the one bottle of champagne, but even so, conversation flows easily. We talk about his parents, my parents, mutual friends. When I ask him more about the development here in Beijing, his face becomes more animated than I've ever seen it. I realize how much of himself he's invested in Saber and how much he adores his job. It's nice to know that my father's legacy is in such good hands.

"This was... nice," I say, as Kent walks me out onto the sidewalk to hail a cab. "Thank you." I'd almost forgotten how easy things are with Kent, how comfortable we are with one another.

"I'm glad you came. I thought maybe you wouldn't."

I can't really blame him. "I'm sorry I've been such a bitch. I don't know what happened – when I became so selfish and spoiled."

"You got in with the wrong crowd. It happens. And let's not forget your father's the one who spoiled you. You, my angel, suffer from only child syndrome."

"You're an only child, too, in case you've forgotten."

"That probably explains why we're both always convinced we're right." He grins. "Come on, let's get you home, before you freeze to death."

Once I'm safely ensconced in the cab, he leans into my window.

"Do you think you can keep yourself out of trouble for the next three weeks?"

"I'll do my best." I'm about to tell the cabbie where to go when over Kent's shoulder, a flash of scarlet catches my attention, and I spot a couple emerging from the Ritz.

The man is elderly, grey-haired and slightly overweight, with a badly fitted suit, and the woman in the gorgeous red dress with the gorgeous wavy hair is – oh my God, it's Mandy!

"Amber?" Kent's eyes are filled with concern. "Are you okay?"

I bob my head, too afraid to move in case she sees me. Kent's body is blocking her view, but Mandy's attention is fixed entirely on her date. She rests her hand on his chest and leans in to listen to something he's saying. Her hair cascades down her back as she throws her head back in laughter, and then they move off down the street and out of view.

"Amber?"

"I'm fine." I splutter, too stunned to comprehend what I just witnessed.

11

My first thought when I wake up in the morning is of Mandy. Okay, technically, it's of Kent – the lingering remains of a very disturbing dream – but I shove that aside. I don't know what's gotten into me. It must be all these weeks without any male attention. I decide that the best way to handle the situation with Mandy is to keep my mouth shut. As Kate said, if she wanted us to know about it, we'd know, and besides, who am I to judge. Instead, once we've gathered in the kitchen for bacon and eggs, which Kate cooks, I fill them in on my dinner with Kent.

"Where did he take you?" Kate asks innocently.

My eyes cut automatically to Mandy, who is wolfing down a piece of toast.

"Some restaurant downtown," I say quickly. "I can't remember the name."

"Isn't he staying at the Ritz?" Kate frowns. Mandy's toast stops midway to her lips.

"He is, but he picked me up."

Pacified, Mandy finishes her crust in one bite.

"Are you ever going to admit you have a thumping crush on this man?" she taunts.

It hits too close to home. "Are you sure you're over the stomach flu?" I ask lightly, "because it sounds to me like you might be delusional with fever."

She and Kate exchange a look, and Mandy grins. It's a smug look.

I HEAD for Mandy's classroom after the final bell. She'd promised to pick up my lesson plans from the admin office, and I want to go over them before tomorrow. On the way to lunch, I hear the sounds of an argument coming from behind her door. Peeking through the glass, fear clutches at my chest. Mandy and a blond man who looks vaguely familiar are head to head having a heated conversation. While I watch, he seizes her wrist, and without any care for the consequences, I barrel through the door.

"Get your hands off her!"

They both whirl to face me, and a look of horrified alarm comes over my friend. The man drops her arm, but he doesn't step away from her.

"Amber," Mandy says, sounding shaken, "this is Mr. Davies... Ryan. He's Jack's dad."

It sounds as if she's expecting me to introduce myself. I don't.

"We'll talk about this later," Ryan tells her. He gives me a brief nod on his way past, and then he's out of the door.

"What the hell was that about?"

Mandy slumps back against the wall, tilts her head back and lets out a frustrated sigh. Then, like a puppet whose strings have been cut, she slides down the wall until she is sitting on her haunches, her head in her hands. I walk over and take a seat beside her.

"You need to tell me what's going on, Mandy."

She sniffs, keeping her face hidden.

"Did he hurt you?"

"No." A soft mumble.

I take hold of her hands and pry them apart. Haunted eyes peer up at me.

"What. Is. Going. On?"

Another low sigh.

"Ryan and I are... we've been seeing each other."

"You're dating him?" The thought of Mandy dating anyone is mind-blowing. I remember the old man she was with last night and a horrible thought occurs to me. "Did he catch you cheating?" I ask, as gently as I can.

"What? No! Why would you say that?"

"I saw you last night," I admit sheepishly. "Outside the Ritz. That wasn't Ryan Davies you were with."

"You saw me? Why didn't you say anything?"

"I figured you must not want me to know. Who was that man? *Are* you cheating? You can tell me. I'm not here to judge you, but I do need answers, especially after what I just witnessed. Are you in some sort of trouble?"

She licks her lips. "It's complicated."

"I'm going to need a little more than that."

"Ugh!" she groans. "I'm an idiot. I thought I had everything all figured out, and then Ryan came along and now it's all gone to shit. Turns out I'm not so good at leading a double life."

I smile. "I'm not one to jump to conclusions, but when you say *double life*, I can't help but think undercover FBI agent. There's no way I can go into witness protection, I've seen the movies, they have bad stylists and get given names like Olga or Peggy."

Mandy bursts out laughing. "Maybe double life is a bit of a strong term."

"Look, you don't have to tell me, but you do have to talk to someone. Trust me, keeping things bottled up is never a good idea. Maybe Kate"

"No." She shakes her head frantically. "Kate isn't like us, she wouldn't understand."

I wait while she deliberates. Then, in true Mandy fashion, she shakes the slump from her shoulders, leaps to her feet and grabs my hand. "If we're doing this, we're going to need Vodka."

TWENTY MINUTES LATER, we are sitting at our usual table at *Calico's*. Mandy orders a double, and downs half of it the second it hits the table. She hasn't said a word since we left the school, but now she gives me a wry grin. "Dutch courage," she says with a shrug of her shoulders, "it's a genuine thing".

I mirror her actions, feeling the burn of too much soda down my throat, and hail the waiter to bring us each another.

Mandy gives me a grateful look. "There is no judgment in this circle, right?"

"We agreed on that a few days into this friendship, and we haven't deviated yet."

"Okay." She bobs her head. "I'm an escort."

My jaw drops. "An escort? Like a prostitute?"

"Oh, God, no! An escort like an *escort*. I accompany people who can't find a date, or who are just plain lonely. I provide company - *nothing* more."

"Okay."

"It sounds odd, I know, but you'd be surprised how many men are craving female companionship."

"That doesn't surprise me at all, but I find it hard to believe they wouldn't want any more than that."

"Oh, some of them do," she admits openly, "but they don't get it. And if they aren't happy with that, they get banned from my books."

"Your books?"

She downs the last of her drink and starts on the second.

"It's sort of a business."

"Mands. It sort of sounds really bad when you put it like that. How did you even get into something like this?"

"I took it over from a girl I met shortly after I arrived here. Cindy worked at the Prada store, and we became friends. She was killing it here – always wearing expensive clothes, lived in a penthouse apartment – well, you know the drill."

"I certainly do," I say, recalling Mandy's lavish lifestyle.

"At the time, I was struggling to afford my rent, let alone designer clothes."

"I know that struggle well."

She grins. "Anyway, one night she said she was leaving Beijing. Her visa was expiring, and she couldn't extend it. Plus, I think she was ready to go home – she lived in the States, too – and she offered me the business. I jumped at it. I was tired of living on cabbage and beer."

"You certainly don't live on it anymore," I point out, with a pang of envy. I may be feeling more fulfilled than I ever have before, but that doesn't mean I don't miss life's creature comforts.

Mandy gives me a knowing look, which tells me she knows exactly what I'm thinking.

"It's not even difficult, honestly. Just a small list of exclusive clients prepared to pay a ridiculous amount of money to spend time in the company of a beautiful woman. When Cindy left, I took over the lease on Cindy's apartment, the list, and that was that. I've been doing it ever since."

"If it's so simple, why are we here? I assume meeting Ryan wasn't part of the plan?"

"Got it in one." She takes another sip of her drink. "I honestly didn't mean to fall for him, but the heart wants what it wants."

"Is he making you give it up?" It's an educated guess, but, to my surprise, Mandy shakes her head.

"Not in the way that you think. Ryan is fine with the business. You really need to believe me when I say it's not sordid in any way," she adds wryly. "Most of my customers are genuinely nice people who lack the social skills to interact with women. I feel sorry for them. I like to think I help – it's like a training course. I equip them so that they're better able to handle women in the real world."

"You're a bona fide saint, Mands."

"Laugh all you want, but it's the truth."

"Ryan?" I remind her to get back to the point.

"Yes, Ryan. I honestly didn't mean to fall for him, but he's so damned charming, and a widower – his wife died when Jack was two – which breaks my heart, and he treats me like a princess."

"It didn't look like that from my perspective." My mood darkens as I remember how he had grabbed hold of her wrist. "He was manhandling you."

She waves my concern away. "It looked worse than it was. We've been going through a bit of a tough time, we're both cracking under the pressure."

"What pressure?"

"Ryan's contract here is coming to an end, and he's moving back to Canada. He wants me to go with him."

I sit back in my chair, stunned. "How the hell have you been in a relationship this serious and yet Kate and I know nothing about it? I mean, I get why you didn't tell us about the business, but why would you keep having a boyfriend a secret?"

"I don't know. I guess I figured when I finally admitted it, it would make it real, and I'd have to make a decision one way or another."

"You're a freaky little weirdo, you know that, right?"

"I am," she concedes. She takes another swig, and I join her. "What do you think I should do?"

"It's not my call."

"I know, but I'd like your opinion."

I think about it. Try to find the right words, and then settle for the most obvious question. "Do you love him?"

She bobs her head, almost embarrassed to admit it.

"Then I think you should go. You'll regret it if you don't."

"Shit. I was worried you were going to say that."

"Then why'd you ask?" I laugh. "Besides, what's the worst that could happen? If it doesn't work out, you could always come back here, or go home."

"I don't think I'd want to come back." She gives me a look more solemn than anything I've ever seen on her face. "I think this is the real deal, Ambs."

"Then you should *definitely* go. What's really holding you back?"

"You're going to laugh at me."

I hold up my hand." I swear I won't."

"It's the business. Not the money," she quickly clarifies, "but the people. Some of these men have become real friends. I'd hate to let them down."

"I'm sorry, Mands, but I can't help you with that. But at some point, it's okay to be selfish and put your own needs first."

"I guess." She doesn't sound convinced.

"Tell me more about Ryan," I say, and the frown lines on her forehead smooth instantly, as I knew they would.

Thankfully, the following morning, Kate is so distracted by the imminent arrival of her fiancé, that she doesn't notice that Mandy and I are unusually quiet. After last night's revelations, my head is still spinning, and after the copious amounts of vodka we'd consumed I have my first real hangover since the night I'd met Ben at the Forbidden City.

Around mid-morning, I receive a summons over the communications system to please see Principal Chen during lunch, so as soon as the children have left the classroom, I make my way to her office.

"Wei's parents have agreed to the private tutoring," Bianca tells me the second I walk through her door. "You can start tomorrow. I proposed Tuesday and Thursday afternoons, right after school, as we discussed. Are you happy with that?"

"Absolutely."

"They're happy to reimburse you privately for your time, rather than through the school, and I think logistically that would be easiest. They're hardly struggling, so I'd recommend you put in a decent fee."

"I wouldn't have a clue what a decent fee is."

She frowns, thinking. "I have a few contacts who are private tutors. Let me get in touch with them and find out. I'll drop you an email as soon as I know."

"Perfect."

I float on air for the rest of the day. Not only am I thrilled that I'll be working with Wei, but my finances just improved significantly. I might even be able to buy myself a little car to get around in.

Mandy throws me a few meaningful looks at lunch, but I have no idea what they mean, and Kate is in a state, constantly checking on Tim's flight details to see if there's going to be any delay.

"When do we meet him?" I ask as she checks her app for the tenth time.

"I was thinking maybe dinner next week? We're going away for the weekend." Her grin stretches from ear to ear.

"No doubt you have a lot of catching up to do," Mandy teases.

"Dinner next week sounds great," I add, as Kate blushes to the roots of her dark hair.

Mandy, I presume, must have a date scheduled tonight, though whether with Ryan or a client, I couldn't say, because she doesn't propose any Friday night plans. I'm happy to get takeaway, which I eat with chopsticks, and go to bed early.

I WAKE up to a loud banging on my apartment door and yank it open to find Mandy on the other side. She's wearing jeans and a Cheshire-cat grin, and her eyes are glittering with ill-concealed delight.

"What did you do?" I ask, catching sight of my watch as I wipe the dried drool off my cheek. She breezes past me.

"I've got it! I've got the solution to all of our problems!" She is speaking so fast I can barely make out what she's saying. "It just came to me, in a moment of brilliance! I, my friend, am a genius!"

"Whatever you've been smoking, I want some," I grumble, as I make my way to the living room and sink onto the couch.

"I'm high on life and wisdom," she replies gleefully, taking a seat beside me. She sits for only a few seconds before she's back on her feet, pacing the small space.

"You're giving me whiplash." I throw a cushion at her. "Sit down, you raging lunatic, and tell me what's going on."

"I think you should take over the business!" she blurts it out without preamble.

I blink, twice. "I beg your pardon?"

"It's the perfect solution! I don't want to let anyone down, and you need the money – no offense."

"None taken," I mumble, intently aware of my abysmal apartment.

"I've given this a lot of thought," Mandy continues, "and I'm deadly serious. You're perfect for this. You're like me... only less glamorous." I look up to find her grinning. "Just checking you were paying attention, you looked like you'd fallen asleep."

"I'm flattered, Mands, I really am, but I don't think I can"

"You can! I know you can. It's a shit ton of money for minimum input. You get free dinner, free drinks. We can even scale down, so you're not overwhelmed. There are a few men in my list who are ready to fly solo, and I'm just spoiling them."

"I can't just pretend to date a bunch of strangers. What will we even talk about?"

"To be fair, they do most of the talking. You just need to sip on champagne and look pretty."

"You admitted yourself that this lifestyle was taking a toll on you – all those evenings out."

"That's because I had Ryan to take into consideration too. And let me tell you, that man knows how to keep a girl up at night."

"Mandy," I groan, covering my ears.

"Sorry, too much information. My point is, you're *not* seeing anyone. And if I'm gone, you're not going to have anyone to party with anyway. You'll be at a loose end most nights." That much is true. Kate never instigates our evenings out. It suddenly dawns on me that

Mandy might actually be leaving Beijing and I feel an inexplicable pang of sadness.

"Have you told Ryan you'll go?" I ask.

"I said I'd try. I'm going to give Bianca my notice on Monday, and I'll leave with Ryan at the end of the month. I'll be back in a few weeks though," she says, catching sight of my crestfallen face. "I have a bunch of stuff to wrap up, and I've told Ryan that if I'm not happy, that'll be my dramatic exit. I just won't go back."

"You'll go back," I say, with complete confidence. She has that look in her eye – one very similar to the one Kate gets when she speaks about Tim.

"Obviously, but it never hurts to keep them on their toes."

"I'm happy for you. But I still don't know if this is a good idea."

"Amber." She sits down and puts her hands on my shoulders "I am doing you a favor. This is a pay-it-forward scheme and you're lucky number three. You've got to get through the year, right?"

I nod. My father was very firm on that. One year, not a day less.

"So, you do this until you're ready to go home. You make a bunch of money, live in a great apartment, and then, when you're ready to go, you hand it over to someone else. Someone *deserving*," she adds, as if this is a great honor.

"Do you have any idea what my father will do if he finds out about this? He'll send me to social Siberia, for the rest of my life."

"Why?"

"What do you mean why?"

She shakes her head. "You still don't get it. You're not doing anything wrong. You've got to get your head around the fact that it's not an *escort* agency, not in the way people think. You're blowing it out of proportion."

I tug my lip between my teeth. She's got a point. I have evenings free, and I can make some real money. It's not like I'm going to be expected to have any physical contact with these men. Mandy pounces on my moment of weakness.

"Just give it a shot," she says. "Go on one date. If you don't believe me after that, we'll call the whole thing off."

"And you'll leave it at that?" I ask, but I'm pretty sure she can already tell by my tone that I'm going to do it.

"I'll never mention it again," she vows.

"Okay, fine. One date, that's all I'm committing to."

"Yes!" she fist-pumps the air. "I knew you'd come around." A wicked grin. "Which is why I already set it up. You better dust off your heels, Miss Holland, because you start this evening."

13

"I am not wearing that."

Mandy and I are in her bedroom. She insisted I get ready at her place, so she could make sure I looked the part, and I'm coming straight back here after my date. Apparently, 'looking the part' requires me to wear an orange and white striped shift dress with a statement gold zipper running down the front. Mandy holds it up against me, checking the size.

"I said I'm not wearing that."

"Orange is Basil's favorite color," she says, not caring in the slightest. "Part of the job is knowing what the client likes, and dressing and behaving accordingly."

"You also said he likes cats. Do you expect me to drink wine from a bowl and meow at him during dinner?"

"Amber," she groans. "Just trust me, okay?"

"I'm not wearing it." I stride across to the closet and start rummaging through it. I've brought nothing with me except my pajamas and a comfortable change of clothes for tomorrow morning. My hands fall on a soft, coral cocktail dress. The color is only slightly more orange than pink, but the fabric is heavenly.

"I'll wear this one."

Mandy tries to stare me down, but I hold her gaze, unflinching.

"Fine," she sighs. "I guess it'll do."

We agree on minimal make-up, though she insists on a bright coral lipstick. I pick out a pair of gold hoops for my ears, and Mandy finishes off the look with a pair of tan heels.

"Fabulous," she announces, after giving me a head-to-toe inspection.

My palms are sweating. "You said he's a doctor?"

"He's a vet. The animal kind."

"Right." I rack my brain, trying to remember everything she told me about Dr. Basil Mitchell in the past few hours. "And he's British?"

She narrows her eyes. "American. Did you even listen to a single thing I told you?"

"Remind me."

She glances at her watch. "We have half an hour. Come with me."

I follow her through to the dining room.

"What on earth is that?" I ask as she dumps a thick file onto the ebony table.

"This," she announces proudly, "is *the book*."

"The book?"

"The book. It's a record of every client – their personal information, likes, dislikes, everything."

I move to open it, but she yanks it out of my reach. With one hand firmly on top of it, she stares me down. "This is the holy grail of this whole business," she says solemnly. "After each date, you should add to it so that the next time they're in town you remember even the small details. That's what makes all the difference."

I try to keep a straight face and fail miserably.

"Okay, A, you sound like a mad woman. And B, when the hell did you become so organized? You can't even keep track of your whiteboard markers."

She throws me a look that clearly tells me I'm not taking this seriously enough.

"Cindy set it up, but I'm not kidding, it's important." She opens it to the front page, and I see a scribbled note right on top.

"What's that?"

She peers at it. Her lips move, and her brow furrows in concentration as she tries to decipher her own writing. Then she rips it out and crumples it in her hand. "Okay, fine, so I'm not as meticulous as Cindy was, but I do keep track of what's important." She flips through to 'M' for Mitchell and finds Basil's profile.

"Here, see," she says, showing me the contents. "Dr. Basil Mitchell."

"Mind if I test you?" I ask. Mandy waves her hand in agreement, and I snatch up the file.

"Hometown?"

"Chicago."

"Favorite color?"

She rolls her eyes. "Orange, obviously."

I run my eye further down the page. "Dislikes?"

"Peas, Celine Dion, and jokes about short people. He's only five-one," she adds, and then, without any further prompting, "Basil has a PhD in Veterinary Science. He visits Beijing every second month to give lectures at the China Agricultural University on his favorite subject – cats – and is actively involved in setting up mobile clinics in impoverished areas to provide basic health checks, vaccinations, and sterilization of domestic felines. He also eats dessert after every meal, even breakfast, and the last time he had a girlfriend was in college. She left him for a plumber named Stan."

I gape at her. "How the hell did you do that?"

"I told you. My clients are nice people. Most just need someone to talk to." She takes the book back. "Oh, and you won't find this in the book, but between you and me, I suspect Basil is gay. He was raised strict Roman-Catholic, so he'll never come out of the closet, but I think he's about as unhappy as a person can be."

"Mandy," I saw slowly, my stomach curling. "I don't think I can do this."

"Don't you dare! You're not backing out on me now."

"Yeah, but... you know these things. You care about these people. I can't do that - I forgot my own mother's birthday, for shit sakes!"

Mandy draws herself up to her full height and gives me a look of pure steel. "Pull yourself together. You are going to meet Basil, and you are going to be charming, and lovely, and so help me if you aren't, I'm going to rip out your arm and beat you with the wet end!"

We're both silent for a long moment.

"That's disgusting."

She grins. "I know. Now move your ass, sunshine, you're going to be late."

WHEN I WALK into the restaurant, I ask for the reservation under Dr. Basil Mitchell. A tall, distinguished-looking maître d, dressed in the customary white shirt and black pants, leads me to the table. I feel like a lamb being led to the slaughter. Fortunately, Basil Mitchell seems just as nervous. He scrambles to his feet as we approach, his round, chinless face creasing into a smile.

It's obvious why he doesn't like jokes about short people. His eyes are dead-level with my nipples as I extend my hand to his in greeting. If mine are clammy, Basil's are slicked with sweat.

"Please," he says, in a surprisingly smooth voice, "take a seat." To his credit, he waits until I'm seated before he takes his own, and then we simply look at one another for a long moment. I try not to stare at the tufts of greyed ginger hair, meticulously combed to hide a horizon of bare flesh.

"I'm Amber," I say eventually, to break the awkward silence.

Basil seizes on this like a lifeline.

"Yes, Mandy mentioned that. Beautiful name, Amber. Like the gem."

"Actually, it's fossilized tree resin."

"Oh." He deflates, and I scramble to recover.

"I always thought it was a gem, too, until my friend Kent informed me otherwise."

He smiles. "Basil is an herb. So I guess we're both named after nature."

I try to laugh, but it's just not funny. Basil's face falls.

"I'm sorry, I'm just nervous," I admit.

"Me too. I know this is a bit unorthodox."

I don't know whether to deny it, or be honest and agree wholeheartedly, but fortunately, Basil seems to have found his tongue.

"When Cindy left, I was so nervous to meet Mandy. Our first dinner was a disaster. She spent the entire evening making derogatory comments about short men," he adds, and I try to look suitably outraged. "But she turned out to be more fun than I ever imagined. She's probably one of my closest friends."

"You must be devastated that she's leaving. I know I am," I say, and, just like that, we find common ground. We both adore Mandy. Her leaving affects both of us, in our own way. Before I know it, the waiter has returned to refill our drinks, and I've all but forgotten that this is supposed to be uncomfortable.

I figure we've exhausted the topic of Mandy, so I switch gear.

"Tell me three interesting facts about yourself, Dr. Mitchell."

"Basil, please. Unless you have a cat at home who needs attending to, I'm Basil to you."

I smile. "Okay, Basil, then."

"Three interesting facts," he murmurs, rubbing his hands together in anticipation. "Let me think. I'm a cat person, but Mandy's probably told you that. Back home, I run a cattery – I look after cats when their owner's travel – and I usually have about twelve or so with me at any given time." He pauses suddenly, his eyes narrowing. "Do you like cats?"

"Love them!" I lie.

"Wonderful creatures, cats," he says, satisfied. "Did you know they're one of – if not the most – popular pets in the world?"

"I did *not* know that."

"Five hundred million people can't be wrong, eh?"

I laugh, and this time it comes out the adoring tinkle I'd planned. Basil warms to his topic.

"Right, next fact. I was born with not one sweet tooth, but an entire mouthful. As you can probably tell." He gestures at his straining waistband.

"Nonsense. You look absolutely fine to me." I know it's the right thing to say by the way his lips curve upward. "Chocoholic," I say quickly, needing to get off the topic. "Got it. What else?"

"I have a deep-rooted love for Asian culture. The art, the architecture, the tradition... I'd spend a lot more time here if I could. If it wasn't for the cats. They need me."

MANDY OPENS the door before I've even knocked. It's only nine-thirty, but apparently, dinner with Basil is never a late affair. I'm feeling pretty good. I've eaten a fantastic meal, had relatively decent conversation, when we weren't talking about cats, and Basil was a true gentleman. He'd walked me out, shaken my hand, and seen me safely into a cab. Not one inappropriate comment or attempt to touch me in any way.

"How did it go?" Mandy asks, bouncing on the balls of her feet.

I dump my purse on the table in the hall. "It went well."

"You didn't screw up?" she follows me into the living room, where I kick off my heels and sink onto the couch.

"I hung onto every feline-related word. He said he was looking forward to seeing me again. Happy?"

She frowns, thinking it through. "You didn't make any short men jokes, did you?"

"Oh my God. No! And that's an improvement from your first date, or so I heard."

"I wasn't warned. So, how are you feeling about it all?"

"I can't actually believe how easy it was. I had fun. And I'm getting paid for it. I *am* getting paid, right?"

"Yes, of course you are! Do you think I'm going to keep taking the money even though you're doing the work?"

"Just checking."

"So, you'll do it? You'll take over?"

"It can't be this easy. What are you not telling me?"

"Oh, stop being such a Debbie Downer. I've handed you the world on a plate, Amber. You should be kissing my feet."

"I feel so sorry for Basil."

"Right? He's a beaut."

"If I could learn to love that nasal laugh, and overlook his height, I'd marry him tomorrow and be Mrs. Amber Mitchell, mother of every ginger cat that exists."

"Don't get too excited, you've only just scratched the surface. And admittedly, Basil is a super easy client."

"Who's next?"

"You're really doing this? You can't back out once you've agreed."

"I'm really doing this." Earning a fortune for being wined and dined? Living in this apartment, with Netflix and no subtitles? I'd be an idiot not to. I run my hand across the satin cushion beside me. "It will be my precious," I say, in my best *Gollum* impersonation.

She grins. "Wait right here. I'm getting the book."

THIS TIME, I'm allowed to examine it. I flip through the thick white cardboard dividers, briefly scanning profiles at random.

"Each profile is filed alphabetically, under the client's last name," Mandy explains. "Don't worry I'll text you the broadcast message list, which has every contact number and name in it. It'll be easier than trying to go through this one by one and adding them to your contacts."

"They'll just text me if they want to see me?"

"Yes. Some will try more often than they're allowed, but don't be shy to get firm with them."

"What do you mean, more often than they're allowed?"

"Oh." She waves her hand in a lazy circle. "The rules. I haven't explained that to you yet. No kissing, no sex, no sleeping over, or even going back to their place. Trust me, it can land you in a whole heap of trouble."

"Are you speaking from experience?"

"Actually, yes."

"You're joking!"

"I wish I was. I slept with one of my clients. I fell for him, hard – thought he was the one and everything."

"What happened?"

"The asshole was married. Trust me, Cindy knew what she was doing when she set the rules." She doesn't wait for me to respond before she continues ticking them off her fingers. "Texting is limited to arranging dates only. And no more than two dates a month. Any more than that and one or both of you might start catching feels, and that's a complication you don't want. Men fall in love faster than they fall asleep, especially when faced with a woman who is literally being paid to agree with everything they say."

"That makes sense." I turn another page of the file to discover a bright red divider. "What's this?"

"That's the red list. Anyone beyond that is a tried and tested asshole. They're either married, or perverted, or both. We don't take on married men, but sadly it's only too easy to take off a ring. If you find out a man has a wife, or a girlfriend, or if he tries anything with you, you shove him in that folder and cut all ties immediately. Don't worry," she adds calmly, "it almost never happens."

While Mandy goes to fetch us a drink, I flip idly through the folder. It's easy to see where Cindy's entries end and Mandy's begin. Cindy was meticulous, her neat, tight handwriting easy to read. Mandy's illegible scrawl, on the other hand, is almost impossible to decipher.

"I have a feeling you're going to be really good at this," Mandy announces as she breezes back into the room with two flutes of champagne.

"I hope you're right. When's my next date?"

"Wednesday, if you're up for it. I can schedule it for you, but after that, I'll send everyone your number and leave it up to you."

"Who's it with?"

"Frank Gunner."

"Sounds like a douche," I say, without consulting the book.

"Oh, you're even better than I thought," Mandy replies and then takes a long sip of her champagne.

14

The next three weeks are a whirlwind. Between teaching, tutoring Wei, and my new business, I barely have time to think, but all too soon, Mandy is leaving and my heart is broken. Kate, who is still coming down from the high of her week with Tim, even now, is taking it surprisingly well. Mandy and I had met Tim during his visit. He was nice. He was Tim. I could understand what Kate sees in him, but he's not my type.

"I can't believe you're leaving," I tell Mandy for the fourth time in twenty minutes. The three of us are standing at departures.

"I'll be back in a few weeks! You won't even notice I'm gone. Besides, you guys at least still have my apartment to drink in. It'll make you feel better." She gives me a discreet wink.

We'd explained to Kate that Mandy would be keeping her apartment, but that I'd be living in it while she was gone. Kate hadn't questioned it. She'd seen my hovel. She sympathized.

"You girls better not get up to any trouble without me."

"As if that would be possible," Kate smiles.

"Right, I'm not into goodbyes, so I'm just going to say see you later and be off, yeah?"

I nod, then, on impulse, I throw my arms around her. Kate does the same.

"Oh God," Mandy mutters, but she hugs us right back.

I'M SO depressed that evening that not even Netflix on Mandy's enormous flat-screen can cheer me up. Kate and I had gone for mandatory drinks after the airport, on Mandy's orders, but our hearts hadn't been in it and we'd left after only two rounds. I'm flipping idly through channels when my phone beeps.

Hi Amber. I'd like to schedule an appointment for Wednesday at 7pm. The Bill and Trout. Please let me know if that works for you. Chase Crawford.

I fetch the book and flip to C. No Chase Crawford. He must be a referral. I haven't had any yet, but Mandy had mentioned this might happen occasionally. Most new clients were sent to us through existing clients.

I don't have anything planned this week, and Kent is only flying in on Saturday, so there's no chance he'll want to catch up before then. Chase's profile picture shows only a man with his back to the camera, swinging a golf club. Hastily, I type a quick reply.

Sure, I'll meet you there at 7.

He sends a thumbs up.

"WEI, THIS IS EXCELLENT!" I exclaim on Tuesday afternoon, as I review the poem he's written. "Really good job, I love how you've compared the sky to a blanket.

Wei smiles. He's been smiling a lot more since we started our private lessons, and it melts my heart every time. Bianca couldn't have been more right when she said that Wei was craving attention. Now that he has it, he's like a different child.

"What do you prefer," I ask him now. "Stories, or poetry?"

"Stories," he answers sheepishly, not wanting to admit this hasn't been his favorite lesson.

"Me too. We'll do another story on Thursday, okay?" I hand him a worksheet. "Now, before you go, can you put these sentences in order for me?"

We are so engrossed in the task that neither of us notices a diminutive, dark-haired woman enter the classroom. When she speaks Wei's name, I almost jump out of my skin.

"Oh my goodness, you scared me!"

"My apologies." She looks to Wei and gives a curt nod of her head before extending her hand to me. "I am Jia Li, Wei's mother."

I scramble to my feet. "I'm sorry, I wasn't expecting you." Looking down at her, it's easy to see where Wei gets his good looks. Jia is beautiful, her thick lashes framing eyes that are so dark they seem to be all pupil. "It's wonderful to finally meet you, Mrs. Li."

She doesn't return the pleasantry, but I plow forward.

"Wei is doing so well. He's really talented. I can show you some of his work, if you'd like?"

"I'm sorry, I'm in a rush." She speaks impeccable English, with no trace of an accent. "Wei, get your things, quickly, please."

"Maybe we could reschedule?" I ask, desperate to engage with her.

"I'm sorry, that won't be possible. My husband and I are moving. Wei won't be coming back."

"What?" My knees threaten to buckle beneath me.

"I've spoken to Principal Chen," she says, as if that settles the matter.

"When? When are you leaving?"

She gives me a pointed look, but I don't give a shit if I'm overstepping.

"It's been quite sudden," she concedes. "My husband's business requires him to go immediately, and I've accepted a transfer."

I glance to where Wei is standing, his backpack over his shoulders. He looks resigned.

"Perhaps I could tutor Wei online? We could continue our lessons remotely. It wouldn't be a problem, most of the syllabus I've set up doesn't require me to be"

"You will be remunerated in full for the notice period," she snaps, and I feel my temper fray.

"This has nothing to do with money, Mrs. Li. I genuinely want to tutor your son. I think he's got an exceptional gift, and I'd love to continue to work with him. You don't have to pay me." I hear myself add.

Jia Li looks at me as if I just crawled out of a block of cheese.

"You would tutor him for *free*?"

I stand my ground. "I would."

She turns to her son. "Would you like Ms...." She trails off, not having a clue what my name is.

"Miss Holland," I say quickly.

"Miss Holland to continue to tutor you?"

Wei bobs his head nervously, unsure whether the honest answer is the right one. Jia gives me an appraising look.

"I'll think about it," she says eventually. "I'll be in touch with Principal Chen if we decide to take you up on your offer." And with that, she turns on her heel and walks out. I reach out and grab Wei as he makes to follow her and crouch low on my haunches.

"You be good," I tell him softly, fighting back tears. This is too soon, too sudden, and I can't quite believe it's happening, but the least I can do is say goodbye. She's not going to contact Bianca. I know it, and Wei knows it too. "You be a good boy, because you *are* a good boy," I say quickly. "And work hard. You're the smartest seven-year-old I know. Don't let me down, okay?"

Wei nods. His dark eyes shimmer but he stands tall, shoulders back. "I won't let you down, Miss Holland," he says.

I sit on the floor, unmoving, for a long time after he's gone.

The following evening, I get ready for my date with Chase Crawford. It's the last thing in the world I feel like doing but, mindful of the exorbitant rent on this apartment, which won't pay itself, I slip on a little black dress and pull up my big girl panties. Bianca had been just as upset by the abrupt turn of events as I was but, sadly, it was completely out of her control.

"His parents have the right to move him wherever they want," she'd said. "And I know this isn't going to make you feel any better right now, but I had to send Wei's transcripts over to the new school. They listened, Amber – it's an exclusive private school with a high-level entrance exam. He's going to be fine."

She was right. It didn't make me feel better.

I CATCH a cab to The Bill and Trout, a cozy little restaurant uptown. The sound of sixties blues wafts through the open door, and I almost walk into the live band.

"Mr. Crawford?" I ask the waiter who steps forward to greet me.

"Right this way." He leads me to an empty table in the far corner of the restaurant. "Mr. Crawford hasn't arrived yet," he says, unnecessarily. "Can I offer you something to drink while you wait?"

"A bottle of red wine, please. The most expensive." I may as well set a precedent for my new client.

"Make it two," a low voice purrs. My head jerks up and my mouth drops open as I catch sight of the breath-taking man standing just behind the waiter. He gives me a crooked smile. "Amber, I presume?"

I recover my composure as quickly as I can with the answer to every woman's fantasy standing before me.

"Chase?"

"Last time I checked." He gives the waiter a wry look. "Just the wine for now." And then steps around him to offer me his hand. "It's a pleasure to meet you, Amber."

I meet his sapphire blue eyes and extend my hand, barely conscious of the waiter scuttling off, dismissed.

"You too."

He takes his seat, draping himself over it like a cat, all lithe grace.

"How did you hear about me?" I ask. "My services, I mean." Even I cringe at the word 'services', but Chase doesn't bat an eyelid.

"Frank."

"Frank Gunner?"

"Do you date *many* Franks?" he asks teasingly.

"Only the one right now."

I don't know if it's losing Mandy, or losing Wei, or just the charisma radiating off him in waves, but I throw caution to the wind. The old Amber opens a sleepy eye and stretches. I know I'm flirting with Chase, which is not against the rules, exactly, but probably not the best idea, given how attracted I am to him. Considering most of the men I'm attracted to end up being the wrong kind, I suspect Chase may not be being entirely truthful.

Half an hour later, my suspicions are confirmed. Not only is he ridiculously good-looking, but he's charming as the devil. We've moved on to our second bottle of wine when I call him out.

"So what's the catch?" I ask, during a rare lull in what has otherwise been scintillating conversation.

"The catch?" he smears a liberal amount of butter onto a bread roll and tears a chunk off with perfect white teeth.

"I wasn't born yesterday, Chase. I've gone on five dates before this one, and seen men so completely unalike they may as well be different species. But do you know the one thing they all have in common?"

"Excellent taste in women?"

I ignore the compliment and fix him with a pointed look. "*None* of them look like you."

He scans his menu. "I should hope not. I pride myself on being the only person who looks like me."

"You know what I mean. Do you really expect me to believe that a man who looks like you can't find himself a date the conventional way?"

"I never said I couldn't."

"Then why am I here?"

He sets the menu down on the table. "I think I'm going to have the salmon. And as to why you're here," he adds, conversationally, "it's simple. I have what I would assume is the opposite problem to your regular clients. I have no problem finding a date. It's finding someone to spend time with who *doesn't* want anything more that's a problem."

I burst out laughing. "You have a problem with being objectified? With women wanting to get you into bed? How very metrosexual of you."

"What can I say? I want to be able to go out with a beautiful woman for once, and make conversation, without it ending in meaningless sex."

"Is that what usually happens?"

He shrugs.

"That must be so hard for you."

"It's a curse."

I steeple my fingers and lean toward him. "Well, Mr. Crawford, I can assure you that won't be happening on my watch. You're quite safe with me."

"And *that*," he drawls, raising his glass in a toast, "is why you're here."

DESPITE CHASE'S CLAIMS, and my best intentions, there is an undeniable chemistry crackling between us. If I lit a match, I'm pretty sure we'd both burst into flames. I drink more than I should, skirt the line between courteous and cute, serious and sexy, and Chase takes it all in his stride. Over and over in my head, I recite the rules Mandy laid out. For all Chase's talk of wanting a platonic friendship, I call bullshit. I don't know what his deal is, but I've been with enough men to know that the way he's looking at me is not the way a man looks at a friend.

"Well, I guess this brings our evening to an end," Chase says softly, as he settles the bill. For the first time tonight, he won't look at me.

My tongue darts out to lick at dry lips. "I guess so."

Chase puts his hand on the small of my back to guide me through the tables but drops it the second we emerge into the frigid night air. For a second, we stand awkwardly, facing each other on the sidewalk.

"Well," I say, brightly, as I extend my hand. "This was fun. Thank you."

His eyes gleam in amusement as he eyes my outstretched hand. I drop it.

"Okay, that was weird. Sorry. I'll just..." I eye the street for a cab. "I'll just go."

Chase's hand catches my arm as I pass.

"Amber"

Our eyes lock. Time freezes. Mandy's warnings fly out of my head faster than a canary out of a cage.

"I don't want to objectify you," I whisper.

"Please, do," he groans, and then his lips crash down onto mine.

WHEN I WAKE up on Thursday morning, it takes a few seconds before the events of last night come rushing back to me. I kissed Chase. I kissed a client. Mandy would be furious, but I don't feel too bad about it. That's all we did. We only kissed. For fifteen minutes, and in full view of the street, but it hadn't gone any further than that. I brush my fingers across my lips. They feel bruised. I haven't done that much kissing since college. Still, it's a good thing that I won't be seeing Chase for another two weeks. That's the rule, and he knows it. It'll give me time to talk some sense into myself. It's not as if I'm falling for him, but who can blame a girl who's been on her own for so long from wanting a little physical affection?

I check my phone to find a message from Mandy, asking how things are going. It's like she knows. I haven't told her about the date with Chase yet, and I decide I'm not going to. It's safer if I don't. For me, anyway. I reply that everything is absolutely fine and ask her how Ryan's doing. *Dragging me to every God forsaken tourist attraction in Toronto*, she replies, but then she sends a heart-in-the-eyes and an eggplant emoji, and I burst out laughing.

ON FRIDAY AFTERNOON, I'm tidying up my classroom, singing Tracey Chapman's 'Give me one reason' softly under my breath, when I hear a deep voice behind me.

"I'll give you one reason to stop singing."

"Kent!" I gasp, my hand flying to my chest. He's lounging against the door frame, looking outrageously casual in a pair of dark blue jeans and a branded T-shirt. He's even wearing sneakers. "What are you doing here? I wasn't expecting you until tomorrow."

"I got an earlier flight. I had an unexpected meeting this morning, so I flew in yesterday."

"How did it go?"

"It went well. What *are* you doing?"

While we're talking, I've started stacking the chairs as I do every Friday.

"Tidying up. The cleaners throw a fit if they have to do more than absolutely necessary."

He smiles, and I know exactly what he's thinking.

"The irony isn't lost on me, either," I remark wryly.

"So this is the place that's tamed the untameable Amber Holland," he says, pushing off the door frame to come toward me. His eyes scan the walls, taking in the children's drawings, and the weekly theme board, which is currently decorated with planets. I stand tall, proud of the work my kids have achieved.

"It's awesome," he says eventually, his eyes coming to rest on me. "What you're doing here is incredible, Amber." I don't want him to see how much it means to me to hear him say that, so I turn my back to him and round my desk.

"You haven't seen anything yet," I say, then adding a hint of my teacher's tone to my voice, "please take your seat, Mr. James."

Kent grins and strolls casually to the desk right in front of mine. It takes him a few seconds to wedge himself into the tiny chair, and I have to bite my lip to keep from laughing.

"You, Sir, are very predictable. Always demanding front row seats."

"Well, I am a star student, so this is where you would place me, not so Miss Holland?"

"That is, in fact, Gabby Martin's desk. Gabby is by far the naughtiest child in my class, possibly the entire school, so you're definitely in the wrong chair, Mister Perfect."

"I'll have you know I was a terror at this age. I blame my best friend. She was always getting me into all kinds of trouble."

"I would've separated you immediately," I say sternly, trying not to smile.

Kent's face softens. "No, you wouldn't have."

"You're right. I wouldn't have."

He scans the other desks. "Where does Wei sit?"

I don't reply.

"Amber?"

"His parents pulled him out." My voice is tiny, fresh pain washing over me.

"Oh, Jesus, I'm sorry." He's trying to get up, but he's having difficulty extracting himself from the chair. "I know how much he meant to you."

"I'm fine. There was nothing we could've done, and he's gone to a really good school. I was just... I wasn't prepared."

"I'm sorry," he says again. He's managed to free himself, but I don't wait for him to get any closer.

"I'm fine, it's over now." I don't want to talk about it. "How would you like a tour?"

To my delight, Kent pays a genuine interest in everything I show him. He asks questions about the children, the teachers, and even asks after Principal Chen's grandmother, who had been ill when he visited three weeks ago.

"She's fine. Bianca was super stressed because they couldn't find what was wrong with her, but it must've been a bug because she bounced back."

We wander back to my classroom door, and Kent looks up at the colorful sign on the door. "Miss Holland's class," he reads out loud.

"That's me."

This time, when he looks at me, it's like he's seeing someone else.

"I haven't seen you this happy in a long time, Amber. I'd forgotten how good it looks on you."

A blush rises on my cheeks. "I am happy." Then, with an arched brow, I add, "but I like to think I always look good."

A low chuckle rumbles from his chest. "That you do."

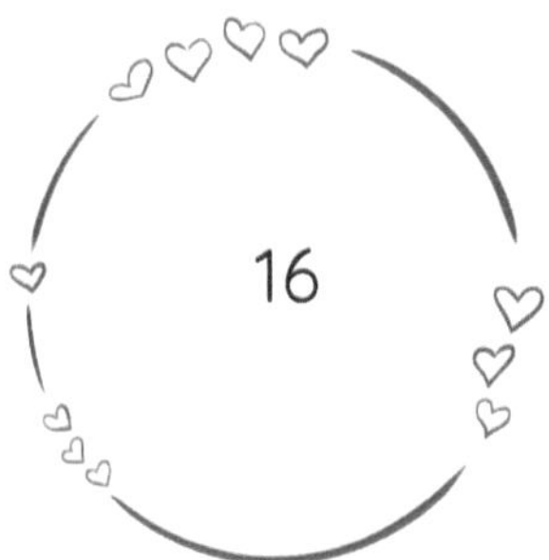

16

I take Kent to *Calico's*, regaling him with the story of how Denri drove us girls here that first time. Given that his hired BMW makes the journey in under a minute, he can't help but laugh either.

"Do you still see much of Denri?"

"No. It took me two weeks to convince him that I was perfectly capable of getting around on my own, but he finally accepted it."

"Do you come here often?" Kent asks as I find us seats at the table I usually share with Mandy and Kate.

"Hey, don't knock it 'til you've tried it," I tease. I try to remember how I saw the dingy little pub the first time I came in here, but I can't. Now, all I see is the cozy wallpapered interior and a bunch of familiar, friendly faces. "You're going to die when you taste the burgers," I add, confidently. "They're the best in town."

It takes Kent ten minutes to get us a beer at the bar, after striking up a conversation with Lorenz, the regular barman.

"Sorry," he tells me, setting two rapidly warming beers on the table.

"Making friends?" I tease.

"I'm a friendly guy."

"You definitely look more approachable than usual. I don't think I've ever seen you in jeans."

"I wear jeans all the time! You wouldn't know because you've only seen me a handful of times the past few years."

I start to tick them off my fingers. "My mom's birthday, my dad's birthday, *your* mom's birthday." I don't mention his father. I haven't seen Kent's dad since his parents split up when we were twelve.

"Christmas Eve," he adds.

"That's at least four times a year."

"My mother would kill me if I wore jeans to one of her functions. Yours too, probably."

Thinking of my mom brings a fond smile to my lips. "I miss her."

"She misses you too. I saw your mom just before I flew out. She said you call her twice a week, which seemed to make her happy."

"I think I talk to her more now than I did when I lived just a few minutes away," I admit. "It's true what they say. You really don't know what you've got until it's gone."

Kent averts his eyes and sips his beer. I'm about to ask him whether he's seen my dad, when my phone beeps. It's a text from Chase, and it catches me so unaware that I almost fall off my chair.

I can't stop thinking about you. It's too soon. He shouldn't be contacting me.

"Everything okay?" Kent asks as I frown at my screen.

I set my phone to silent and shove it back into my purse. "Everything's fine."

We eat our burgers in silence. Kent admits that he's never had better, which gives me a smug satisfaction, and then we head back to his hotel for a few drinks. On the cab ride over, I point out a few of my favorite places – the street-side market which sells the best wontons in town, the holistic center, where Kate, Mandy and I had medicinal leech therapy, which, I add, is as gross as it sounds.

"I got this," I say, holding up my arm to show him a small, fresh scar on my elbow, "in that park. I fell off my bicycle," I add, as he scans the flash of green to our left.

"Were you drinking?" he asks, but his voice is filled with humor.

"I wish. Mandy insisted we race down to the river. My only consolation is that she fell off, too."

"She left, right?"

"Yes. It's not really the same without her."

"Sounds like you've had a bit of a bad time. First Mandy, then Wei."

"That's life, I guess."

We walk into the airconditioned lobby of his hotel and make our way to the bar. A few finely-dressed patrons give us odd looks, and it takes me a while to realize that they're offended by our casual clothing.

Kent orders us each a beer, and then he deliberately raises a toast to a blonde woman who is still openly glaring.

"You're terrible," I laugh. "Maybe you should go upstairs and put on a suit."

"Screw that." He gives me an appraising look. "Actually, I have a better idea. I'm not in the mood for this pretentiousness. Let's both go to my room." He orders a bottle of wine to be sent up, while I stand stock still, mixed emotions barrelling into me. I know he means nothing by it, but the thought of being alone with him in his hotel room does something to my stomach.

"You coming?" he asks when he realizes I'm not following him.

"Right behind you!" I shake myself and step into line behind him.

KENT IS HILARIOUS. I'd forgotten how funny he is. Away from the prying eyes of fellow guests, we lounge on the enormous twin couches in his room, drinking wine and gossiping as if we're back in high school. The wine warms me from the inside out, but it's Kent who keeps the heat in my cheeks.

"God, I've missed you," he says after I've performed an Oscar-worthy impersonation of Erica Gilmore, his college girlfriend, which included a deep and meaningful conversation with the potted plant beside me. He's laughing as he says it, but it makes my heart flip-flop in my chest. I don't know what's happening to me.

"I need to use the bathroom," I say, grabbing my purse.

Once I've locked the door safely. Behind me, I. whip out my phone.

I'm with Kent, I text Mandy. *And I'm having feelings. Help*!

I stare at the screen, frantically trying to calculate the time difference, and almost weep in relief when I see that she's typing.

I'm not understanding your problem.

It's Kent!

The hottie from the photograph?

Yes.

And you're with him now?

Yes.

Is there a bed in the general vicinity?

I frown. *Yes.*

I'm still not understanding your problem.

I should've texted Kate.

"WOULD YOU LIKE A REFILL?" Kent asks when I walk back into the living room. He's sitting exactly where I left him, but the TV is on, volume turned low.

"No, I'm good, thanks."

He switches the TV off.

"Actually, I think I should go."

"Go?" he blinks at me. "Why? It's still early."

"I know, but I have a busy day tomorrow. Lesson plans and all that jazz."

"Okay." He gets to his feet, looking disappointed. "I'll walk you out."

"You don't have to do that. I can see myself out."

"Don't be ridiculous."

We don't speak in the elevator ride down to the lobby. Kent is searching my face, but I keep it blank, revealing nothing. The street outside is quiet, but the second we reach it, Kent's control frays.

"Amber." Kent runs his hands through his hair. "What's going on?" He's standing close to me, too close, and even in my heels, I have to crane my neck to look up at him.

"Nothing." I duck my head, but his hand rises to my chin, and he tilts it back. I blink in embarrassment under his scrutiny.

"Don't lie to me."

A lifetime passes between us. His eyes are warm, filled with concern, and it hurts to look at him.

"You were right," I admit softly.

"About what?"

"It wasn't Erica. It wasn't just you. Back in college," I add hastily, as a look of confusion crosses his face. "I pulled away first. I got involved with Lara, and that stupid crowd, and I lost track of what was important."

He blinks, taken aback by my admission. "You're saying I was important?"

"You were my best friend, Kent. Of course you were. You..." I shake my head, my thoughts in turmoil. So quickly, so easily, we've slipped back into this familiarity, as if the past few years never happened. But they did happen, and Kent – Kent grew up. He grew up into a successful, incredible man, and I was too self-absorbed to notice. I'm the world's biggest idiot.

"What did you mean?" I ask, frantic for a handle on my emotions. "When you said that you dated Erica because she was interested."

"Amber..."

"I want to know." I'm firm because it's been niggling at me since he said it, and I need to know if my suspicions are founded.

His eyes burn into mine. Neither of us looks away. A cab ventures near, but he makes no move to hail it down. My heart starts to beat a little faster in my chest.

"What do you think I meant?" he murmurs eventually, and the resignation in his voice is as good as an admission.

I feel pinpricks of pain in the corners of my eyes. "Why didn't you tell me?"

His sigh is soft and sad. "Would you have cared?"

I don't need to say anything. We both know the answer. I want to apologize, to tell him that I was stupid, and selfish, and blinded to what had been right in front of me, but it's too little too late. And I'm terrified to ruin this fragile new peace between us, to jeopardize the friendship we're so carefully rebuilding.

"I care now," I whisper, so softly I'm not sure he's heard me.

"Amber." My name is a song on his lips. His arms come up, reach for me, and then they fall away. Kent's expression is one of horrified regret. "Amber, there's something you need to know."

I barely register the words which follow. Only that her name is Megan, and they've been seeing each other for a few months. My jaw aches with the effort of keeping my expression neutral, and my heart slows to a dull thud.

"I'm happy for you." I hear myself saying, my voice too high, too bright. "Really, Kent, I am."

A puzzled frown. "Amber, I"

"That all happened a long time ago," I say quickly. "We're different people now. I just wanted you to know that I'm sorry for how I treated you back then, that's all. Mostly, I'm just glad we're back to being friends."

"Can we go back upstairs?" he is pleading. "We can talk about it."

"There's nothing to talk about." I spot a lone cab cruising down the street, and I leap forward to flag it down.

"Amber!" he yells after me.

"Thank you for a wonderful evening," I call back, and then I launch myself into the cab.

17

I'm not proud of what I do next. Humiliated and heartsore, I text Chase. *What are you up to?*

Nothing right now.

Want to meet for a drink?

His reply is only one word. *Where?*

We meet at a pub just a few blocks down from my apartment. It's tiny, but the jukebox in the corner belts out eighties love songs and drowns out the sound of my phone ringing. Kent has called four times, but I don't answer.

"I must admit, I was surprised to hear from you," Chase says when he arrives. He kisses me full on the mouth in greeting. "I know I wasn't supposed to contact you for another two weeks, but I've never been good with rules, and I certainly didn't expect a reply."

"I'm not particularly good at following rules either, obviously."

He tips his glass toward mine, "To rule breakers."

I force myself not to think of Kent. He's not available, and I'll be damned if I let that come between us now, after we've finally managed to become friends again. The best thing to do is move on, as quickly as possible. Chase is a nice guy. He's successful and funny, and someone I could see myself falling for. So I focus on what's right in front of me. On the present, because there's no point living in the past.

THE FOLLOWING MORNING, I get a text from Kent. *Flying home, something's come up. I'll be back as soon as I can. We need to talk.*

I hope everything's okay. I reply. *We can talk when you're back.*

When he follows that with a phone call, I don't answer it.

I DON'T HEAR from him for two weeks. In that time, I have a platonic date with Basil Mitchell and one of Mandy's other regulars – James Gerber – a giant of a man with a mop of curly hair and the creased face of someone who's spent a lifetime working outdoors. I also have five very non-platonic dates with Chase. The more I spend time with him, the more I start to believe that he could truly be the man who gets me over Kent. I'm aware that I've been avoiding Kate, but she's too nice to comment, and I know that right now I have bigger issues to deal with. Mandy, on the other hand, is not as tolerant. Only two days ago, she'd torn into me on a video call for not keeping in contact. "I'm flying in on Sunday," she'd warned, "and I expect to see your face!"

I don't mention that Saturday is my birthday. I don't tell anyone.

ON SATURDAY AFTERNOON, Chase and I watch a movie at the local theatre, most of which we miss because we're making out in the love seat.

"Can I come back to your place?" he asks as the credits roll, his voice a warm breath in my ear. I stiffen. He hasn't been to my apartment. I haven't been to his, either. We've done a lot of kissing, but our relationship hasn't moved beyond that. To be fair, we've only had eight dates. The old Amber would be laughing her twisted head off. The new Amber is far more conscious of her reputation.

I gaze up into Chase's blue eyes. They're warm and inviting.

"Sure," I say, as his mouth finds mine for another lingering kiss.

Outside my apartment block, he raises both brows and gives a low whistle.

"Business must be good," he teases.

"Well, seeing as I haven't charged you a cent, you should be grateful that someone else is footing the bill." That's another good thing about Chase. He doesn't judge me for what I do. He understands that none of my other dates are any threat to what we have.

He chuckles, his fingers interlaced with mine. His thumb massages the palm of my hand in slow, lazy circles and my pulse spikes. I know what he's expecting, when we get upstairs. I smile at him, trying to slow the frantic beating of my heart as we head for the elevator. Chase seems to sense my unease. He starts kissing me, sweetly, before the doors have opened. I melt against him, feeling his strong hands on my hips, the long, lean length of him pressed up against me. By the time we reach my door, our kisses have become deeper, more urgent, and I fumble behind me, trying to get my key into the lock.

"SURPRISE!" The roar of raised voices sounds the second we tumble through the door. I drop my keys and leap away from Chase, my hand rising to cover my mouth, my shoulders heaving as I gasp for breath. A stunned silence follows as I take in Mandy, Ryan, Kate, Bianca, and my parents standing in the hall of my apartment. I take them in with one quick sweeping glance, but it's the tall, dark-haired man at the end who draws my attention. The man who is gazing at me with a hollow expression, his eyes filled with pain and disappointment. He tears his eyes away from me to look at Chase, and then he shakes his head.

"Kent!" I say as he stalks past us. I don't even bother explaining to

Chase as I rush after him. "Kent!" He's standing at the elevator, jabbing the call button with unnecessary force, his head bowed. "Please look at me."

I don't expect him to obey, so when he does, I'm still trying to find my words. "Where are you going?" I ask lamely.

He laughs, but it's a horrible sound. Dry and bitter.

"What's wrong?"

He doesn't reply, just jabs again at the button. I feel a flare of anger rise in my chest. Sure, having everyone see me and Chase making out isn't ideal, but Kent's reaction is completely irrational. Especially seeing that he has a girlfriend.

When the elevator doors open, I step right in beside him. He jabs the button for the ground floor. "The least you can do is talk to me," I snap.

He rounds on me in disbelief. "Oh, really? Like you've been talking to me the past few weeks?"

I flinch away from the genuine rage on his face. "I wasn't ignoring you. I've just been busy."

"I can see that." The words are cold and ugly.

"That's not fair! This is ridiculous, we're friends. Why are you acting like this?"

"We're not friends, Amber. Not anymore."

"What?"

"Two weeks ago you said things, things that implied you felt something for me. *Two weeks ago*. And I believed you!" That harsh bark of laughter again. "God, I'm an idiot. All these years. People don't change, I don't know why I let myself believe that you had."

"I have changed!"

"Two weeks ago, Amber!" he roars, so loudly that the elevator doors seem to rattle. "You couldn't wait two weeks before you jumped into bed with another man!"

My head jerks up. "Wait? What do you"

"Forget it."

The elevator doors open, and he steps out. "Happy birthday," he sneers, handing me a ribbon-enrobed envelope. I take it, automatically, and gaze up at him, at the muscle going in his jaw, at the cold fury in his green eyes. "Goodbye, Amber."

All the way back up to my floor, I stare at that envelope, wondering what the hell just happened. It doesn't make any sense. I slide my thumbnail under the seal and tear it open, but before I can reach inside, the doors open and the sound of furious voices reaches me.

Mandy and Chase are standing in the hall outside my apartment, clearly involved in a heated argument. There's no sign of anyone else, and I can only pray they're all still inside.

"What's going on?" I say when it becomes obvious that Mandy and Chase haven't noticed me. They both turn to look at me, but Mandy gets there first.

"What the hell are you doing, dating this sack of shit?" Mandy demands.

"I beg your pardon?"

"Chase Crawford!" she seethes. "What's the point of the book if you're going to ignore everything inside it?"

"What are you talking about?" I ask, risking a glance at Chase, He doesn't look angry. In fact, he looks... amused.

"The red list," Mandy says. "This bastard's on it."

"No, he's not," I say, shaking my head in emphasis. "I checked. There's no Chase Crawford on file. He's a new referral..." I trail off as I catch sight of the ugly grin spreading over Chase's face. "You're a new referral," I repeat, but this time I speak directly to him.

"Afraid not, sweetheart."

My blood is thundering in my ears. "I don't understand."

"He's married," Amber spits out, then, giving me an apologetic look, "this is the guy I told you about. The one I broke the rules for. He's a lying, two-timing pig."

"You're married?" I gasp, but Chase isn't listening. He reaches out a hand and brushes his fingers across Mandy's jaw. She slaps it away.

"You girls have your little games," he murmurs, sparing me a wink. "And I have mine."

"Get out," I snarl. "Get out, you son of a bitch, or, I swear to God, I'll rip your fucking dick off."

Chase takes two swaggering steps toward the elevator when I draw back my fist and send it hurtling toward his face. Pain blossoms in my knuckles, but I feel the satisfying crunch of bone beneath it.

"You bitch!" he clutches his bleeding nose.

"Try explaining that to your wife," Mandy drawls.

Chase rounds on her, his arm raised, and for a heart-stopping moment, I think he might hit her.

"Try that, son, and it'll be the last thing you ever do." My father speaks from the now open doorway, the Great White on full display. The predatory look on his face is terrifying. Chase backs up, and I press the call button for the elevator. It opens immediately and swallows Chase whole.

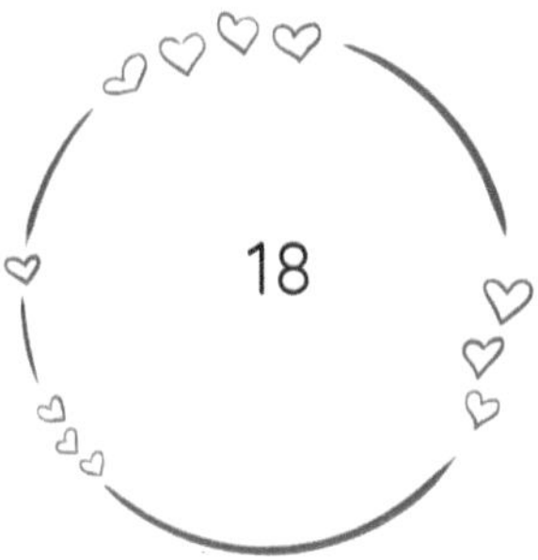

18

It takes the better part of an hour to explain everything to my parents. There was no lying my way out of it – the apartment speaks for itself – something Mandy forgot to consider when she planned this surprise party. After Chase had left, she took everyone downstairs for a drink so I could speak to my parents in private.

"I don't understand why you'd do it," my dad insists. "If you needed money that badly..."

"Dad, seriously. I'm not a whore. It sounds bad, but it's not like that. And I didn't want your money. Well, I did, in the beginning, but after I started working and cut back on the booze, I started to enjoy the financial freedom. I know this isn't exactly the ideal way for you to be introduced to my life here, but it's been good for me. You were right. It's exactly what I needed."

"Kent told us," my mother says quietly. "That you were flourishing here. He's been keeping us informed."

I try not to wince at the mention of his name. "See? You know Kent wouldn't give me credit if it wasn't due."

Even my father can't fault this reasoning.

"And that man?" he asks. "The one outside. How does he fit into all of this?"

"He's just an asshole who conned me into thinking he was something that he wasn't. Don't look so stressed, dad, we didn't actually sleep together. And even the most responsible people make mistakes. What happened today with Chase doesn't take away from all the good I've achieved here."

He seems about to question me further when his pocket beeps. "It's Kent," he says, reading the incoming text. "He's catching the next flight out of Beijing."

They both look up at me as the blood drains from my face.

"Sweetheart," my mom says softly, "what happened with you two?"

"I don't know. Everything was going well, but then today... he just lost it."

"It can't have been easy for him, seeing you with that man," my dad grunts. "I know it wasn't easy for me."

"Dad, Kent and I are friends, but it's got nothing to do with him who I date!"

"She's right," my mom says, and I give her a grateful smile. "I think your father and I are just confused, Amber. From what Kent was saying, we thought perhaps you two were more than just friends. Or on your way to being more than friends, at least."

"That would be a bit difficult, considering he has a girlfriend."

Their eyes meet, and something passes between them.

"What?" I ask. "What are you not telling me?"

"Honey, Kent doesn't have a girlfriend. He did," she adds quickly, "but he flew home two weeks ago to end things. Megan was devastated, and it took her a few days to accept it, but he explained that his heart belonged to someone else. We were under the impression that *someone* was you."

. . .

I HOLD it together until my parents have retired to my guest room, their jetlag finally catching up with them. Mandy returned about an hour ago, after dispatching all the other guests, including Ryan, home. They're staying in a hotel just a few blocks down. Mandy has barely spoken since the confrontation outside, but once my mom and dad have said their goodnights, we take a seat in the living room.

I heft the book from the side table and dump it on her lap.

"Show me."

Mandy flips through it, the furrows on her brow deepening with each passing page. When she reaches the last divider in the red section, she raises her head and gives me a look of wretched apology.

"I must've thrown it out," she says, in a voice heavy with remorse, "God, Amber, I'm so sorry. I hated him so much. When I found out the truth, I must've ripped it out of the file."

"It's not your fault," I sigh. "He must've known you were gone, and he took a chance. It paid off, obviously. There's no way you could've known."

"I might've, if you'd confided in me," she points out.

I give her a weary smile. "I'm sorry I didn't tell you. I'm sorry I've been quiet. Things have been a bit crazy."

"I know you were upset about Wei leaving. And then something happened with Kent?" It's an educated guess, given what went down earlier.

"Oh God, don't remind me." I cover my face with my hands, briefly, and then force myself to look at her. "I don't even know how this happened. One minute he was the bane of my life, and driving me nuts, and the next..."

"You wanted to jump his bones?"

"Well, yeah."

"I hate to break it to you, Amber, but you've been crazy about that man since the day I met you. I don't know who you thought you were fooling."

"Myself?"

"Good job. You're the only one you managed to convince."

"What am I going to do?"

"You're going to live out the ending of every romcom you've ever watched. You're going to go after him. And," she adds wryly, "you're going to do it without subtitles."

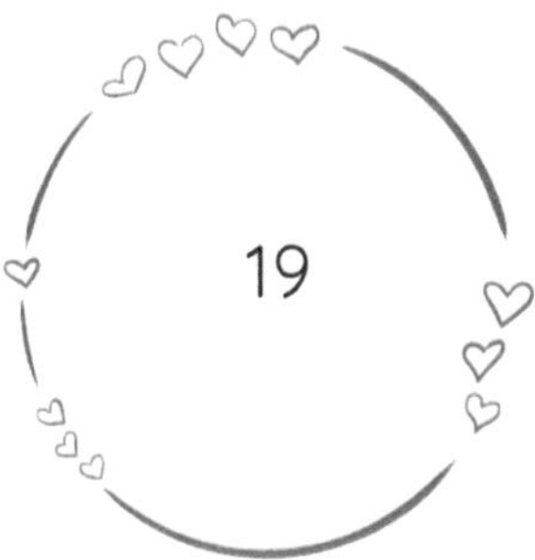

The dry heat of the Santa Ana winds hit me in full force the moment I step off the plane. My father had temporarily lifted his ban on my spending to secure me a first-class ticket home to "sort out my shit," as he so eloquently put it. I know that he only did it because it involves Kent. I could tell by the smug look. Nothing would make him happier than to see me end up with the man he already considers a son. And, for the first time in my life, what he wants and what I want are perfectly aligned. I grabbed the ticket. I didn't even offer to pay for it myself.

Bianca had accepted my excuse that there had been a family emergency, in her stride, but I only had three days. I'd be returning to Beijing, with or without Kent.

The cab ride to his apartment is the longest of my life. I keep my eyes on the road, the miles flashing by in a grey and white blur, while my heart races in my chest.

"Thank you," I say when we finally pull up outside Kent's apartment block. I hand over a few crumpled bills. "Keep the change."

I brought nothing with me, save for my purse. I have enough clothes in my apartment to last a lifetime, let alone a couple of days, and, thanks to Amber and the lucrative second income she passed along, my credit card is good to go.

I stop only when I reach Kent's door. I didn't think to call ahead, and for all I know he's not even here, but I still need a minute to compose myself. What he saw, back in Beijing, isn't going to be easy to explain. The escort business may be innocent, but my relationship with Chase was definitely not.

I'm trying to find the right words to explain it all when the door is yanked open, and Kent bursts from his apartment, in an obvious hurry. Eyes fixed on his cell, oblivious to the fact that I'm standing here, he knocks me clean off my feet, and we go down in a painful heap.

"Jesus, Amber!" he yells, disentangling himself and getting to his feet. "Are you okay?" He offers me his hand and I take it. We face each other and I notice the dark shadows under his eyes, and the empty look within them.

"What the hell are you doing lurking in my doorway? There's a bell, you know."

"I know. I'm sorry, I was about to knock."

His gaze slides over me, from head to toe and back again. "You're sure you're okay?"

I nod.

"What are you doing here?"

"I came to see you. We need to talk."

"Really?" he crosses his arms over his chest. "About what?"

I glance up and down the hallway. "Could we go inside?"

"No. Whatever you have to say to me, you can say it right here."

"Kent."

He doesn't budge.

"Fine! What you saw yesterday, it wasn't what you think. Wait," I add quickly, "it's exactly what you think, but I can explain."

"I'm listening."

"Chase is... was, someone I met before you and I had dinner that night, but we weren't together. Not until after you told me you had a girlfriend."

"Do I look like I was born yesterday?"

"It's the truth! Nothing happened! We haven't even... you know."

"No, I don't know." He is not going to make this easy for me.

"We haven't had sex!" I snap, loud enough that he winces. His eyes travel the length of the hall, and he curses under his breath.

"Get in here," he mutters, holding the door wide. I scuttle inside. We head for the kitchen. Kent starts making a pot of coffee, with unnecessary force. "Explain."

I do, in fits and starts, tripping over my words more than once. I leave nothing out. At some point, Kent hands me a mug of coffee, but he doesn't speak, only stands opposite me over the marble island and listens.

When I'm finally done, I look up at him. Kent's face is unreadable.

"Your coffee's cold," he says.

I blink in confusion. "What?"

"Your coffee," he says simply, reaching over for my mug. "It's cold."

"That's all you have to say?"

"No. I have a lot to say, but I'm trying to get a hold of my..." he trails off, turning away from me so I can't see his face.

"Your temper?" I prompt. "You're trying to get a hold on your temper?"

Only when his shoulders start to shake, do I realize he's laughing.

"What the hell is so funny?" I storm around the island and walk right into his personal space. His eyes are streaming, and he sets down the mugs to wipe at them with the sleeve of his shirt.

"Only you," he says, between gasping breaths. "God, you're a mess."

I don't take it too personally, though, because his arms have come around my waist as he says it. I press my lips together to keep from laughing too.

"It's not funny," I say.

"You're right," he sniffs, composing himself. "And you may be a mess, but you're *my* mess." The possessive pronoun sends a thrill through me.

"You're really not mad at me?"

His face softens. "I'm really not mad at you. I've spent the last few years of my life watching you self-destruct, Amber. What you've done... well, it might not be the most conventional way to do it, but you've stood on your own two feet." He smiles down at me, and his arms tighten, shifting me into the space between them, snug against the length of his body. "When your dad sent you over there, I was convinced you'd be back in a week, broken, and broke. Instead, you not only rose to the challenge, but you embraced it. I couldn't be prouder. I'm sorry I didn't hear you out," he adds, "but seeing you with Chase..." I feel his hands tighten convulsively at the base of my spine and, for a second, his face falls. "You're sure you're not secretly in love with that bastard?"

I rise onto my toes, so our faces are only inches apart.

"The only bastard I'm secretly in love with," I say, speaking slowly and clearly, "is you."

His eyes blaze with triumph. It's a beautiful sight, but I don't have time appreciate it, because his head dips and my eyes close automatically as his lips meet mine.

FIRST CLASS never so looked good as it does now, with Kent lounging in the seat beside me. His hands are constantly seeking me out – they stray to my hair, my thigh, trace small patterns at the nape of my neck.

"My lucky charm," he says, as the air hostess brings us each a complimentary glass of champagne. I grin at him over my glass.

"Is this real?" he asks, and I know exactly what he means. It's all happened so quickly, and yet, taken us a lifetime to reach this point.

"I hope so," I say. "You know, you could've saved us a lot of time and hassle if you'd just admitted you were in love with me back in college."

"You would've run for the hills."

"Lara would've dragged me." Thinking back, I wonder if Lara didn't suspect all along and, fearful of losing her party sponsor, had driven that wedge deeper between us.

"Speaking of Lara. Have you spoken to her at all since you left?"

"Once. She made it crystal clear that I wasn't any use to her without my platinum card."

He gives me a knowing grin. "I hate to say I told you so..."

"Bullshit. You live for it."

He leans over to kiss my nose. "Is it wrong to feel so ridiculously happy after everything that's happened?"

"If it is, I'm just as guilty as you are."

His lips find mine, and he holds the kiss slightly longer than is appropriate, but the flight hostess only gives us a fond smile.

"There are a few things we need to clear up, though," Kent murmurs into my neck.

"Hmm, like what?"

"Well, if you're serious about staying in Beijing and seeing your year out, I'm thinking you should give up that apartment and get a key to mine. Saber has enough invested in Beijing to justify me staying too."

"Give up my apartment?" I fake mock outrage. "After all the work I've put in to get it?"

"Oh, you mean eating at fancy restaurants and drinking all the expensive champagne your heart desires?"

"Yes. That's exactly what I mean. I don't think you appreciate how difficult it's been for me, Mr. James. It's a tough job, but someone's got to do it."

"Well, I guess we better start looking for your replacement. I don't want to tell you how to live your life, but I would prefer that I occupied your evenings from now on." He squeezes my leg and a blaze of heat rockets up my thigh.

"I'm sure we can come to some sort of arrangement," I say, trying to keep my voice light. "I mean, there should be a discount for frequent users."

His low rumble of laughter is music to my ears. "And I plan to use you frequently."

I rest my head on his shoulder and draw the blanket up over us.

"I'm sure there'll be someone to take things over. Mandy's replacement is single, and I caught her eyeing up my Prada boots last week." I tilt my head to breathe in the trace of aftershave on his jaw. "Are you sure you want to stay in China? You've worked so hard. I'd hate to think that you're giving up other opportunities because of me."

"Amber." He shifts so that I have to raise my head to look at him. "I only work so hard because I thought it might get your attention. I only throw my heart and soul into your father's business because I know, ultimately, it's all for you. Trust me," he adds, dropping another kiss on my brow, "I'm never leaving your side again."

"What if my dad decides I need to learn another lesson, and sends me to Siberia?"

"Then I guess I'll have to get a warmer coat."

EPILOGUE

Of course, my dad wouldn't send me anywhere. He was so thrilled about Kent and I, the only place he wanted us was back home. To his dismay, we refused. I was seeing out my teaching year, come hell or high water. It meant too much to me, this sense of accomplishment, and Gabby Martin had started to show an interest in poetry, of all things. Besides, I couldn't let Bianca down. Mandy's replacement, Molly, was only too happy to take over the escort business, but, unlike Mandy and I, she resigned from the school within two weeks when she realized how much money she stood to make. I'd handed her the book, with Chase's updated file in the red list. Kent had laughed his handsome head off when Basil Mitchell had called me to tell me he approved.

Now, with less than a week left, we're packing up the apartment which we've come to call home. I have my heart set on a west coast wedding, and Kent's mom has threatened to disown him if we don't get our arses back to the States before Christmas. So, I'm finally headed home. A new Amber. A better Amber. With the man I love by my side. But first, we're making a short pit stop. There's a wedding in Canada that I wouldn't miss for the world.

ABOUT THE AUTHOR

Rachel Rhodes is a pseudonym for award-winning author, copywriter, and lover of the written word, Melissa Delport. She is published in both S.A and the U.S.A and offers professional copywriting services and author coaching.

For ten years she owned and operated her own specialized logistics company until she woke up one morning and decided it was time to put her English degree to good use.

Melissa lives with her husband and three teenagers, none of whom take her seriously.

She also writes romantic suspense as Lissa Del and contemporary romance as Rachel Rhodes.

For more information, visit www.melissadelport.com

ALSO BY RACHEL RHODES

ROMANCE & ROMANTIC COMEDY (as Rachel Rhodes)

Awkward in Print

Awkward Abroad

Awkward Infidelity

Awkward in Trouble

CONTEMPORARY WOMENS FICTION (as Lissa Del)

Rainfall

Riven

A Life Made of Lava

URBAN FANTASY

GUARDIANS OF SUMMERFELD SERIES

The Cathedral of Cliffdale (Book 1)

The Fight of the Fallen (Book 2)

The Hope of Hawkstone (Book 3)

The Balance of the Blood (Book 4)

Full Series Boxed Set (Books 1-4)

SHADOW MAGIC SERIES

The Witchborn Curse (Book 1)

The Shadow Huntress (Book 2)

The Charmed Quarter (Book 3)

The Rogue Coven (Book 4)

The Darkest Realm (Book 5)

The Hybrid's Fate (Book 6)

Full Series Boxed Set (Books 1-6)

THE TRAVELER DUOLOGY

The Traveler (Book 1)

The Survivor (Book 1.5)

The Saviour (Book 2)

TIME TRAVEL FANTASY

The Clock Keeper

DYSTOPIAN

THE LEGACY TRILOGY

The Legacy (Legacy Trilogy Book 1)

The Legion (Legacy Trilogy Book 2)

The Legend (Legacy Trilogy Book 3)

ANTHOLOGIES

The Space Between Dreams & Chaos

The Space Between Magic & Mayhem

www.ingramcontent.com/pod-product-compliance
Lightning Source LLC
Chambersburg PA
CBHW020912310726
48980CB00011B/857/J

* 9 7 8 0 6 3 9 8 4 4 8 6 2 *